Midwife in the Jungle

Fiona McArthur

Jonah

'Jonah. Can you hear me?'

Jonah Armstrong groaned as he surfaced through the fracturing thinness of his delirium towards the distant sound. There was something about the cadence in her voice that calmed him. Something that made the ghosts fade and lose potency.

The nightmare receded as he eased out of the strangling mists and opened his eyes a sliver as he tried to focus. Even his eyelids hurt when he cracked them and the struggle with their weight felt too great. The face of the speaker hung surrounded by a halo of light, which seemed reasonable for an angel, and she must be an angel because he didn't recognize her.

And he was dead.

Jonah's tongue shifted stickily on the roof of his mouth as he tried to speak. His lips opened and closed. The halo approached as she brought her face closer to catch his words.

'Melinda's ring.' His voice came out barely a whisper, fractured and uneven.

'There is a ring on your finger, Jonah.' Softly. Calmly. Her voice.

He sent the message to his brain to lift his eyelids again, but the synapses weren't listening. The peppermint of her breath touched his face. Did angels chew peppermint?

'Jonah, the airline ticket in your wallet says you flew in from New Guinea two days ago. Are you taking antimalarials?'

This time his muscles obeyed, and he could discern her eyes were dark and caring. His sluggish brain finally articulated his answer. 'Last night. In pocket.'

The angel slid her hand into his trouser pocket, retrieved the tablets and read the label. Then she stepped back from the bed and spoke to someone. 'If it's malaria, presumably this strain is resistant to Doxycycline. We'll just have to try something else,' she murmured.

Everything went black. Time passed. The ghosts returned.

When Jonah regained consciousness, he accepted he hadn't died. Too many aches for death. Close thing. Eyes forced open, he stared at the tiny square of light coming from behind the edge of the curtain as if it were a signpost to the normal world. Tentatively he stretched his legs, and although the ache pulled and resisted in his muscles, the flooding pain of movement from yesterday had subsided.

Warily he turned his head on the damp pillow as someone approached his bed. Still fuzzy, he squinted to bring the woman's two heads together. Once they'd fused, he could see she had the darkest brows he'd ever seen above brown eyes filled with the compassion he'd heard yesterday.

So, she wasn't an angel. Angelic, but real.

'Good morning, Dr Armstrong. I see your fever's broken.'

Jonah swallowed and licked his lips as he tried to form the words his brain had trouble framing. She must have noticed because she moved swiftly to the bedside table, picked up a plastic tumbler of water and directed the straw into his mouth before he even figured out his desperate thirst.

He sighed as the coolness slid down his throat and the roof of his mouth no longer tasted like the entrance to a bat cave.

'Thank you.' His voice cracked with weakness and he despised the sound. Still, it was better than being dead.

'Your strain of malaria was a particularly vicious one and I thought for a while we were going to lose you.'

He could tell she was genuinely glad he was awake, and the knowledge warmed the last of the cold spots in his body. Being alive was good. He'd survived tropical snakes, spiders and crocodiles in the depths of New Guinea only to succumb to a mosquito in the height of civilization. The idea vaguely amused him.

'And you are...?' He could feel the strength seeping back into his limbs and there was sweetness to the feeling. A stark reminder that he shouldn't take his body for granted. He'd done that for far too long.

'Jacinta McCloud. I'm one of the doctors from the emergency department here at Pickford.'

She smiled and suddenly he felt light-headed again, but this time for a different reason. The old barriers refused to assemble as he'd trained them. Blame the malaria – or fate, or timing – because there was something about this woman that slid like a stiletto straight to the core of him in a way he hadn't experienced before.

His life did not include women you couldn't leave behind!

Almost as if she sensed his panic, she turned away and walked to the window. He watched the way she moved, her back ramrod straight like Sister Angelina, the solitary missionary nun he'd grown up around in New Guinea. Yet somehow, it didn't come off. She couldn't hide the fact she was unmistakably a woman.

And there he was again, speculating about someone outside the parameters of his life, and he didn't do that. Angry with himself, he pulled his disgustingly weak body upright past the pillow until the cold backboard of the bed was hard against his spine, and he had control.

Jacinta

Jacinta McCloud, Director of Emergency at Sydney's Pickford General, a mid-size teaching hospital, could see in her mind the man's large, capable hands and the finely wrought signet ring on his little finger. Yesterday she'd seen the tiny butterfly fashioned from gold on the signet. She shivered at the memory and rubbed her shoe over her ankle where her own tiny tattooed butterfly hid unnoticed.

She felt as agitated as this patient had been yesterday, and impulsively she swept back the curtains to allow the morning glow to flood the room. When she slid the window open, cool air damped the heat in her cheeks, and memories of her first sight of Jonah Armstrong ran through her mind.

Pushed through the casualty doors by the ambulance personnel, he'd been agitated by the movement of the trolley and she'd spotted him immediately. He'd mumbled semi-audible phrases and the depth of his despair had radiated from him like an aura. Compelled to comfort, Jacinta had slipped her fingers into his hand to ease his trip to the assessment room. An action odd and personal, something she couldn't remember doing before with an adult.

Strangely, he'd seemed to rest more easily on the bed at her touch, and when the stretcher stopped and she'd retrieved her hand, he'd twisted his head on the pillow as if searching for the respite he'd known too briefly.

The imprint of his long fingers on hers had burned with more than the man's fever. Not the sort of fanciful notions she was known for.

Then, last night at home when she'd turned out the light to go to sleep, his tortured blue eyes had haunted her. Almost as if she'd imagined they had some deep connection, which was bizarre, as she was the least fanciful person she knew. Whims and past lives had no place in Jacinta McCloud's busy schedule and neither did malarial-stricken mystery doctors who blew into the Emergency department. It was probably just the lure of tropical medicine that piqued her interest, not the man.

The breeze from the window tickled her face and brought her back to the present. She'd needed to open the window to create space between them, but now the strength of the sun made her wince. And goodness knew what it would do to Jonah if his eyes were still sensitive to light.

Funny how she thought of him as Jonah and not the Dr Armstrong on his file. Her fingers balled to pull the curtains again, confused by the thoughtlessness of her actions.

'Leave it open.' His voice held a tinge of harshness that made her turn and face him. He sat upright with his broad chest facing towards her like a teak tree-trunk dissected by a curling trail of fine dark hairs that disappeared down under the sheet. If she was noticing things like that, it was time for her to leave.

She moistened her lips. 'Well, I'm glad you're feeling better. You probably won't see me again as I only dropped in on my way to work to find out how you woke this morning.'

How inane. Jacinta winced and her voice trailed off. This was unlike her. She smiled in the general direction of the bed and averted her eyes as she walked towards the door.

'Call me Jonah.' His voice followed her, the rough edges softened, and she was drawn against her will for one last look. 'Thank you for looking after me, Jacinta.' His voice softened, teased her with tendrils of humor and friendliness, and she couldn't look away.

He was smiling and she hadn't seen that before. Wished she hadn't seen it now. He changed completely when his white teeth flashed and his square chin softened; crinkled eyes and the self-mocking amusement in his eyes circled her in his warmth. She couldn't help smiling back. A smile that took flight like a bird out of her serious mouth.

She needed to fly away, not genuflect like an idiot at him.

'You're welcome.' Thankfully her voice came out calm. She focused again on the door because she had to get out of there before she sank into a chair and just stared at him, dribbling.

'And is there a Mr. McCloud?'

Good grief. Was it mutual? 'I could tell you but then I'd have to kill you. You've been my patient.' She glanced back. A beam of sunlight glinted off the butterfly on his little finger, and with his tousled hair he looked a little like a pirate. The wicked satire in his eyes amused Jacinta and she looked away to stop herself from laughing out loud. She felt like she'd just downed a glass of champagne – or two.

'I see you're feeling much better,' she murmured.

He persisted. 'And the answer would be?'

She looked back at this man who should be barely conscious, flirting with her as if it were his last two minutes on earth.

'Yes, there is.' She paused. 'My father. Though technically he's a doctor and not a mister. Now I must go.'

'At least drop by this afternoon, Jacinta, and tell me how you treated my illness.'

To create a reason to return tempted mightily and she should be confident she was level-headed enough to be intrigued without danger. 'Perhaps. I may be running late. We'll see. Goodbye, Dr Armstrong.'

'Dr McCloud.' He returned her formality and nodded with that supreme confidence good-looking men had. You knew, they knew, they'd made an impression.

Jonah

Jonah watched the door shut behind her and although he listened, he couldn't hear her footsteps. Quiet walker. But why would he want to hear her increasing distance?

The smile on his face seeped away and his shoulders slumped into a more relaxed position as he closed his eyes. 'Don't go there, Jonah.' He shook his head at the impossibility of the thought. The selfish stupidity.

Instead of the oblivion of sleep, which he craved, Jonah saw the caring warmth in the dark brown eyes of Jacinta McCloud, and he knew that somewhere in his chest a need he'd never allowed had surfaced. The ramifications terrified him, but not for himself – for Jacinta.

After the loss of his mother and sister, Jonah had accepted that his road would be a solitary one, but already this woman had infiltrated his resolve in a way he would never have believed could happen to him.

He opened his eyes again and stared at the door. Perhaps she wouldn't come this afternoon and he'd never see her again. A thought almost as terrifying as the first. He shifted in the bed and wondered cynically to what lengths he would go to seek her out despite knowing he shouldn't. He was in deep trouble.

Moving quietly down the corridor in her sensible shoes, Jacinta couldn't help glancing up at the clock. For the first time ever she was late for work. She compressed her lips and stepped up her pace.

One of the reasons she'd been appointed as Director of Emergency at such a young age was her reliability. This was all the more reason to stay away from Jonah Armstrong this afternoon.

Jacinta

Fate conspired against her and for the second time in two days a patient with severe headache, fever and chills presented, but this disease baffled them. Malaria tests came back negative, as did those for dengue fever and meningitis. The only clue Jacinta isolated was what appeared to be a black-crusted bite, a bite the man's wife said had started as a red mark about a centimeter wide, or almost half an inch, nearly a week ago.

She followed the case when the elderly man, Mr. Ross, became critical and was transferred to Intensive Care. Insidiously her brain suggested that perhaps Jonah Armstrong might have an idea what the problem was.

It was a good enough reason to stand outside his door at five-thirty in the afternoon. Only 30 minutes late off duty at the end of her day. Still, she hesitated.

The door opened before she could knock and Jacinta took a step back in shock. Jonah Armstrong stood in front of her, albeit swaying slightly, but still he towered over her and the wall of his chest was imposing at close quarters. She stepped back even further. Lying in bed, he hadn't seemed so big!

When she realized she'd retreated, Jacinta lifted her chin and raised her eyebrows. 'Are you supposed to be out of bed?'

He blinked and she thought again how beautiful his blue eyes were and that was when she knew, without a doubt, she shouldn't have come.

'Good afternoon, Jacinta.' Her name rolled off his tongue as if he'd been practicing it, which was ridiculous.

Then he, too, stepped back and gestured grandly for her to enter, like some old-fashioned butler. 'I'm so pleased you could visit as I may go berserk with my own company in here.'

'I could arrange for you to be moved to a four-bed ward, if that would give you the social stimulation you require?' Thankfully her brain still functioned in some capacities. Still, compelled against reason, Jacinta walked past him into temptation.

'I was thinking more like discharge into the real world, but let's put all that to the side and just enjoy each other's company.'

Jacinta had pulled herself back in control. 'I haven't come for the company, I've come to pick your brain.'

'Even better,' he said, as he gestured for her to sit while he climbed back up onto his bed. He couldn't hide his weariness as he lay back, and Jacinta frowned. It was obvious he wouldn't appreciate her repeating that he shouldn't have been out of bed.

'I understand you've worked overseas a lot and have a background in tropical diseases.' She'd asked about him and one of the nurses knew more than she expected.

He nodded so she went on. 'We have a patient with severe headache, body temperature over forty degrees Celsius, a purpura rash, chills and generalized adenopathy. The only other characteristics seem to be a lesion on his right arm that is now crusted with a black scab and even more marked axillary lymph enlargement.'

She looked up to see if he had any suggestions, but he gestured for her to go on.

'He's heading to crisis. His pulse rate is going up, blood pressure's coming down and we're getting some muscle twitching and delirium. His condition is now critical.'

He had his hands behind his head and she could tell he was running through the possibilities in his mind. 'Has your patient been to the forest? Did he have a cough?'

'I think his wife mentioned a cough earlier in the illness and they've been back from Northern Queensland for a week.'

Jonah nodded. 'He's probably been brewing it for a week or more. I'd check him for scrub typhus or tropical typhus. The scab's the give-away. It's from a mite bite and subsequent larvae. You will have to watch for myocarditis, but the illness responds well to Chloramphenicol or Tetracycline.'

Just like that. His knowledge was impressive. Though she didn't delude herself that was all the attraction he held for her. So now what excuse did she have to stay? 'Thank you. I'll pass your thoughts on to the intensive care physician.'

Jacinta stood because she really should go, but one question wouldn't hold her up long. 'How long have you been involved in tropical diseases and medicine?'

He smiled, almost shyly at first, but the promise in it rose like the sun until that gloriously wicked grin captured her full attention. His feet swung over the edge of the bed again so that she wasn't standing over him while his intense gaze travelled her face and neck as if to assess her real interest. Jacinta hoped this was the full extent of his charm because already she was having trouble dragging her eyes away from his face.

'My sister and I grew up as MKs.'

Concentrate, Jacinta, she mocked herself, but it was hard not to just watch his lips without listening.

'Missionary kids,' he explained when she shook her head, puzzled by the abbreviation.

His voice had dropped to a deep rumble and Jacinta accepted that his rich tones fascinated her. She could have watched-listened to him all day. Not only because his background fascinated her. He fascinated her.

'MKs have unusual childhoods,' he said with a crooked smile. 'And think it's normal to be one of the only English-speaking people for miles around.

'There're drawbacks, though. Some of the food I've eaten would never appear on a menu, and the general level of hygiene leaves a lot to be desired. As a doctor you see diseases in such an advanced state you can't believe the human body could still move, let alone have just trekked so many miles to see a doctor.'

He shrugged but his eyes burned with commitment and she could see the real man now.

'My passion is not just for tropical diseases but the progress of diseases in the tropics. I keep going back because otherwise someone else would be even more stretched for time with one less pair of hands. And I do believe I can help.'

Jacinta nodded, aware he'd skimmed the surface of his reasons, and aware also how much she'd love to listen to him talk more of his experiences.

Warning to self: leave now.

Except she didn't heed that warning. She needed to hear more. 'I understand that Papua New Guinea is politically unsettled at the moment. What about the danger?'

'I'm used to that environment. MK, you know, so it doesn't bother me.' He paused, eyes serious and fixed on her. 'It would be different if it weren't just me. It's too risky to have a family in some of the places I visit. My father found that out after my mother was killed.

'I wouldn't say that it's too dangerous to work there.' He smiled without humor. 'But it's no place for a non-native woman.'

She wondered about the ring on his finger. And the name he'd murmured. Melanie? Melissa? Melinda? That was it. Melinda's ring.

He lifted his head and steeled his expression as if to ward off the dark memories. Those blue eyes looked right into her. 'How about you? Did you fall into this profession or were you always going to be a doctor like your daddy?'

The question came out more indulgent than mocking but either way she didn't like it. She said flatly, 'I didn't know my daddy until I was seventeen and thought myself an orphan. So, no, it didn't come from him.' The intentness of his gaze compelled her to go on. 'Like you, I saw something when I was younger that made me want to be able to prevent unnecessary death where I could. By then, later, it was easier that my father is wealthy and a doctor as well.'

She omitted the fact that the woman had been her own mother dying in childbirth and that as an orphaned teenager she'd lived in poverty for the next year before her father found her. The other loss she dared not disturb. Jonah didn't need to know those things.

And she'd spent enough time with him. 'I have to go. Thank you for your suggestion about typhus. I'll pass it on before I leave.'

'Will I see you tomorrow?'

He continued to watch her, unsettling her with his interest. Instead of looking back she glanced at her watch and she couldn't believe how much time had passed. 'I don't think so. Look after yourself.' She smiled her professional smile in his direction and then concentrated on getting out the door.

When she left the hospital ten minutes later she'd contacted the new patient's doctor with Jonah's provisional diagnosis, and further tests were ordered. She hoped definitive treatment would soon be started and the extra confusion she now carried about Jonah Armstrong had been worth the trouble.

She'd tossed her white coat hurriedly onto the tiny back seat of her red convertible, an embarrassing but fun gift from her father as a graduation present, and kicked her shoes off as she settled into the driver's seat. Then she retracted the hood, something she'd never done before at the hospital carpark, and let the heat out in one go.

Jacinta smiled as she weaved in and out of the peak-hour traffic with the wind in her hair. There was something sensually liberating about driving home like this, with her hair shifting in the breeze and her toes in direct contact with a responsive gas pedal. Why had she been so determined to always be restrained and responsible? It had just never struck her she could be this woman.

She bumped over the ridge where her driveway met the road. Her house was one of many in the circle of pastel painted clones in an upmarket development she'd been recommended to buy for capital growth. She tapped her fingers as she waited for the automatic garage doors to open.

Something shifted at the curtains and she saw her cat prowling the front windows behind the curtains – used to, but still cross, at Jacinta being late.

Her mobile phone rang as she let herself into the house, and Moggy, her half-grown Siamese, wound its legs around hers in disapproval at the lack of attention. Moggy was in for disappointment, though the cat should be used to volunteer Wednesdays. Jacinta had half an hour to eat before she had to go out to the youth refuge.

She plucked her phone from her bag on the way to the fridge. It was her stepmother, Noni, and Jacinta pressed loudspeaker and sat the phone on the bench. She lifted the sealing plastic wrap from a pre-packaged meal and paused to glance at the calendar before she slid the dish into the oven. It must be nearly time for Noni to descend for her monthly stopover.

'Yes, I had a good day. How're Dad and the kids?'

Noni's throaty chuckle echoed down the line. 'Fine, but we haven't seen you for ages. I'd like to come down next weekend to visit if that's okay.'

Jacinta smiled. 'When is it not okay? I thought you must be due for a stay.' Jacinta could feel the familiar guilt creep over her.

Noni would have preferred Jacinta to drive to Burra for a change, but the trip down to the Riverina of New South Wales always made Jacinta's heart ache to return to the place where her happiest memories were held in timelock with her loss.

Burra contained all the best memories of Jacinta's life after her single mother died and her father had found her. Memories also of those magical few weeks with her infant daughter, Olivia, before they discovered she had the same congenital heart defect that had killed her mother.

Olivia succumbed, and after her tiny daughter's death Jacinta never forgave herself for not caring more during her pregnancy, despite the assurances of everyone that Olivia's condition had been predetermined. As a final farewell, she had a tiny butterfly tattooed on her ankle in memory of her daughter.

Then, with her father and stepmother's support, she'd thrown herself into study determined to become a doctor. Her off-duty hours were spent at a teenage refuge where she formed friendships with many young women going through the same troubles she'd faced before the father she'd never met had found her and taken her to Noni.

Though, lately, her stepmother had been hinting that Jacinta should look for another life apart from commitment to work and welfare, and her stepmother had begun a campaign of gentle harassment.

Take up travelling, get a pet. Jacinta looked across at the sky-blue eyes of her cat and shook her head ruefully. Noni's words flowed over her as Jacinta-the-doctor turned into Jacinta-the-stepdaughter.

'When are you due for a holiday?' Noni asked.

'I can't take a holiday. You gave me a cat.'

Noni chuckled again. 'We can mind the cat. You need a break.'

Jacinta would have loved to have seen her father's face when Noni said that. He was not a cat person, to put it mildly.

Her smile faded. She couldn't see herself as a lady of leisure. The last ten years since she'd moved to Sydney had been such a rush with university, then the long hours of residency, then even longer hours as Emergency Registrar at Pickford, until she'd finally earned her position as Director of Emergency.

To be appointed Director had been her ambition, and she'd followed it single-mindedly, like everything else she'd done since the death of her daughter. She'd assumed she would be in that job for a long time to come, so why did she feel so suddenly unsettled?

She didn't know what to do with free hours more than once a week. She glanced at the clock. Today was turning into a day that was characterized by her being late.

Jonah Armstrong's face insinuated itself into her mind. The day had been characterized by something — or someone — else as well.

'I met an interesting man today.' She didn't know why she said that, but the silence at the other end of the phone confirmed that she had. She winced at the speculation that statement would cause, so hurried on before Noni could form any questions. 'Give my love to everyone. I'll ring you later tonight if I get home at a reasonable hour, but I have to go now.'

Jacinta put the phone down, opened the screen door and let a bell-collared Moggy out for a few minutes before she crossed the hall to climb the stairs. She noticed the plant Noni had given her last month was wilting badly. She really must water it.

Her father had often said she tried to jam too much into her life, but Jacinta had no doubt that life played fickle. She was covering her bases. He hadn't been there to watch Adele kill herself to feed and clothe their daughter.

Maybe Iain McCloud wouldn't have allowed their hardship if he'd known of his daughter's existence, and he had been there for the last twelve years, but Jacinta wasn't prepared to take from him forever.

It was almost a penance to her mother that, although she had joined the ranks of the wealthy when her father found her, she'd decided to rely only on that wealth until she could stand on her own two feet.

She could certainly do that now.

Her father had a new family to be responsible for and Jacinta loved them. But they were hours away and his family, not hers. Olivia had been her family.

She glanced around at the home she'd made and finally realized she'd met her own expectations. The trouble was today, it seemed, she was rattling around among her own possessions.

She was a twenty-nine-year-old, fully qualified career woman with a healthy savings account and the freedom to do what she wanted.

With empty days and hollow nights.

Jacinta sank into her chair and stared out the window, dinner forgotten on the bench. She'd achieved what she'd set out to do so why was she so unsettled? Why today?

How could she jolt herself out of the doldrums?

Jonah

'Tropical diseases and travel.'

Jonah Armstrong shrugged his shoulders. He didn't notice all the nurses sigh as if he'd taken off his shirt like a tennis player at the change of ends. He saw Jacinta arrive for work and smile grimly as she caught the conversation. She pretended not to see him.

'Dr McCloud.' Jonah pretended no such thing. 'Just the person I was looking for.'

As a signal to break up a gathering, this worked well and the nursing staff drifted away with only a few backward glances.

She looked him up and down critically. 'I gather you're well enough to be discharged today.'

'I'm perfectly well thanks to this wonderful establishment.'

Those dark intriguing brows of hers rose. 'In my opinion you look just fair, with a faint yellowish tinge to your skin. Still no doubt, this time anyway, you'll shake off the lingering effects from the fever if you take it easy enough.'

He heard the unspoken next time you may not be so lucky. Did she care, he mocked himself? Wouldn't that be nice. 'I won't be hitting the pub and abusing my liver for a while, if that's what the appraisal was for.'

He must have been remarkably close to the mark because this time she did smile.

'Hopefully you'll give it a month before you fly anywhere with new parasites.' Despite the smile her voice came out as dry as his mouth still felt.

To hell with beating around the bush. 'I won't be rushing out of Sydney for the next couple of weeks. I'd like to see you again. Though I understand that you could be reluctant to give a stranger your phone number.'

He'd startled her enough to make her meet his eyes. Good. She had beautiful eyes.

'You know where I am, Monday to Friday.' Her voice was cool and even. After he'd been so brave.

When you fancied someone and they didn't return the attraction, you had the raw end of the stick, but he couldn't stop himself pushing for a little more. But Jonah kept his tone measured. 'I was thinking about the weekend. If I hear of any interesting tropical diseases, can I give you a call?'

She looked away and laughed and then looked back at him. Threw out her hands. 'I can't help but be intrigued by the life you must have led while I've been rushing from home to work and back again. Compared to you, I'm dull.'

His turn to laugh. 'You're not dull.' He saw her withdraw a little with that and contrarily it made him keen to find out why.

She said, 'I don't understand how I've piqued your interest.' Then she shrugged. 'It's unlikely you'll catch me but perhaps we'll manage to get together before you go back to your next adventure.'

Jacinta glanced away to the emergency entrance and he turned his head to see what she'd seen. The administrator who'd introduced himself to Jonah this morning waved and started towards them.

Jacinta frowned. Jonah picked up the hint and held out his hand. Crashed and burned. Probably for the best.

Thankfully before the other man could get too close, Jacinta weakened.

'Try white pages online. J McLeod. Bondi. I have a landline I keep for emergencies.'

Felt the smile inside grow. 'Thank you.' He pulled a card out of his pocket for the medical corps he worked for and transferred it into her palm. 'If you have a tricky fever like yesterday, feel free to give me a call or e-mail me. Try the mobile, and if I'm around I'll be more than happy to discuss the case with you.'

Her fingers curved around the card gingerly. 'Thank you. I'll put you on the file as a resource,' she said as the other man came up beside her.

Jonah smiled blandly at them both, but he saw the moment the sound of approaching sirens cleared him from her mind. She wasn't feeling what he was. Obviously. Maybe he wouldn't try to contact her at all.

When Jonah returned to his hotel room and threw his keys on the cheap pine hallstand, he felt chilled by the impersonal look of the room. He really should make a permanent base in Sydney to call home.

But first he'd ring his employer and give himself a couple of weeks' sick leave because the last thing they needed was for him to become delirious a hundred miles from the nearest airstrip and die on them. It would be too much work for the staff.

It wasn't the first time he'd contemplated establishing a home in Sydney, but this was the strongest he'd felt about it for a while. He could always leave the house to the mission when he died. He'd spent the last ten years flitting around the world, staying with friends for short breaks and in hotels when he felt antisocial.

Most of his off-duty time he'd spent hunting up supplies and endorsements that kept the tiny hospital in Papua New Guinea that he'd befriended from closing. He didn't actually own a home where he could have his own things around him and put his feet up without having to be polite to anyone.

He grimaced at the unattractive picture of himself he'd just painted. He could sell a few of those shares his father had bought for a rainy day and still live well off the dividends. Then he could lend the house out to colleagues who needed a break.

He had a handful of friends who were property developers but he'd have a look for himself first.

Tomorrow, when he had more stamina.

There was something about Sydney he enjoyed, more so after this morning, and he wondered just how much was to do with a certain dark-haired, dark-browed, dark-eyed doctor.

It was funny how clear Jacinta was in his mind and the thought brought a frown to his face. It was unlike him to be persistent towards someone who didn't know his rules.

He'd long ago decided to avoid serious relationships, and despite the growing tourist industry, he was still under the opinion that New Guinea was too isolated to take a family to live. Melinda's ring reminded him of that. He winced as the familiar guilt twisted his gut and he stroked the gold on his finger. They'd been so idealistic and foolish and his sister had paid the price.

He was too old to change his ways and become a regular worker like that administrator fellow at Pickford who'd been making eyes at Jacinta.

Unable to sit with his thoughts, Jonah stood to pour himself a drink then remembered his joking promise to Jacinta that he wouldn't abuse his poor liver for a few weeks. He smiled cynically and replaced the tiny bottle of Scotch in the bar fridge before taking himself off to shower away the dark thoughts.

Depression was a normal sign after a serious illness, he mocked himself.

The next morning Jonah began to scan the real estate section of the internet on his laptop. It was funny how his eyes were drawn to those properties for sale in Bondi.

Jacinta

On the Sunday of the following week Jacinta heard her phone ring, and Noni, Jacinta's stepmother, down for the weekend, picked it up.

'Jacinta, it's for you. He says his name is Jonah.'

Jacinta sucked in her breath and glanced in the steamed mirror. Saw the confusion in her eyes. How was she to deal with this? She'd spent the last week reassuring herself he wouldn't ring.

He was a FIFO in town for a few weeks. At best she'd be a diversion for him and at worst she could fall for the guy. Not what she needed.

Stop it. Was that really a danger? In a week or two before he disappeared again? Unlikely. He was interesting and she really did want to find out more about his work.

Risky but attractive. 'Okay. I'll be there in a minute.' She pulled the towel from the rail and wrapped it around herself, then turned the tap on again to rinse cold water against suddenly hot cheeks.

She hadn't thought he would ring.

Noni's voice drifted up to her. 'I think he was on a mobile because it just cut out.'

Jacinta sagged back against the vanity and closed her eyes. Maybe it was a sign, though she didn't believe in signs. If he rang again she'd say she was going out for the day. This much confusion from one phone call could only spell trouble. He probably wouldn't ring back.

The sound of the doorbell five minutes later had her heart bounding in her chest. She'd always wondered what palpitations felt like. And she'd bet it was Jonah Armstrong that showed her.

'Do you want me to get that?' Noni called out from the kitchen, and Jacinta didn't know what to do.

'I'll get it,' she said, and dashed into the bedroom to pull on a sundress that didn't require a bra to be modest.

It was her fault that Jonah had turned up at the house. She'd been the fool who'd told him she was in the white pages.

She dragged a comb through her hair and whipped the back of it into a ponytail.

The doorbell rang again and this time there was no comment from Noni.

Jacinta trod slowly down the stairs and across the hall, and she paused before opening the door to look through the security peephole. It was Jonah all right and he looked as good as she remembered.

She opened the door and glared at him. Though in truth it wasn't him she was cross with. 'I'm not impressed at you just turning up, Dr Armstrong.'

She scowled at him but he looked gorgeous. He must have been fresh out of the shower too. He had weight to regain to flesh out his face, but she was thrown by the way his damp hair curled over his really quite sexy ears.

Since when were ears sexy?

She had to physically restrain herself from asking if he was eating enough. Though why on earth that fact was interesting she didn't want to consider.

He held out his hand apologetically. 'My phone died and I was outside when I rang.' He shrugged. 'It was an impulse to call you. I'm looking at a house in the next street and hoped you might come with me.'

'I'm still not impressed at you turning up uninvited,' she repeated but felt herself relax as he smiled.

'It's the ladies of the house.' He spread his hands helplessly. 'They regard me suspiciously if I come on my own. I think I need a chaperone.' He glanced into the house behind her. 'You could bring the lady I spoke to on the phone with you?'

Jacinta narrowed her eyes. 'My stepmother is visiting for the weekend.'

And going through her pantry throwing out expired stock like she did every time she came. Jacinta always found it amusing – because she didn't care if things had expired and ate them anyway. Probably because she'd been hungry in her youth and food was food. She still found it near impossible to throw anything out.

He took a step back and surveyed her. 'I really did want to ring you first to check if it was okay to call around but my phone died before I could get to you.'

'Hmmm.' Jacinta glanced at her wrist but she hadn't had time to put her watch on. 'We're going out shortly.'

He looked at his own watch. 'It's nine o'clock and I'll only take a few minutes of your time.'

Why was it so important she went with him? Obviously he was very reluctant to lose. She couldn't remember the last time such a pursuit had mattered to her.

'Oh, all right,' she relented. 'Come in and I'll grab my phone.'

He grinned at her less than gracious invitation as if he'd scored one point for the male of the species, but waited for her to enter first.

He followed her into the house and she wondered fleetingly what he saw.

Jacinta's home was open plan, very feminine and restful with lots of cane and soft lounges. Magazines were scattered across the coffee-table and a couple of terminally ill house plants wilted quietly in the comer.

'I see you have a green thumb. I don't know why I find that appealing, but I do.'

Was he flirting with her? She looked at him from under her brows and scowled at him again. 'It's my forte.'

Jacinta stopped at the bottom of a curved staircase, called towards the sound of someone stacking dishes. 'Noni, could you come through for a minute, please?'

Jacinta introduced him. 'Noni, this is Dr Jonah Armstrong. He's down from New Guinea for a few weeks and wants my company while he looks at some real estate. Apparently,' she glanced at Jonah and then back at her step-mother, 'the house is in the next street so I won't be long.'

Noni smiled, her mobile face easily drawing a return smile from Jonah and held out her hand as if she'd known him for years. 'It's lovely to meet you, Jonah.'

Jacinta watched Noni glance up and down the full height of him and she even patted his hand. Lord, she hoped Noni wouldn't invite him for lunch the way she was eyeing him. Jonah looked smitten, too.

She stepped between them as she picked up her small clutch with phone and purse. 'I'll be back soon.' She hugged her stepmother and turned to Jonah. 'Lead on, Dr Armstrong, and I'll look at this house with you.'

The home they inspected stood perched on an impossibly steep block with an overgrown jungle anywhere that wasn't bare rock, but inside it had magical views out to sea from a turret window and the front veranda.

The previous owner had even set up a telescope, and the furnishings in the house weren't far from nautical either. It was a man's home and there wasn't a lady of the house to be seen anywhere. So much for requiring a chaperone!

Jacinta rolled her eyes. 'Imagine coming here without a woman,' she muttered sotto voice.

Jonah seemed to be spending more time looking at her than the property he was supposedly interested in, but she had to admit to enjoying herself hugely. Jonah's sense of humor had her giggling when she least expected it and there was something off-beat about the house that made her wonder if it wasn't perfect for him.

The crusty executor officiously showed them over the property and each corner held a new curiosity. The house was being offered with contents, and for a man with few possessions it was an easy way out for Jonah.

When they returned to the car Jonah was silent as he drove her home in his hired vehicle.

Jacinta glanced across at his profile but she couldn't read his expression. It was strange to be sitting across from a man she barely knew after something as personal as looking at real estate together. She wondered what he was thinking.

'Well?' she prompted. 'What are your thoughts on the house?'

'Fine.' Jonah stared straight ahead. But there was something in his voice that made her think of him two days ago, ill, and barely conscious in the hospital. Which was ridiculous as he looked perfectly healthy today.

She frowned. 'You don't sound happy?'

He took his eyes off the road for a second and glanced at her with a rueful smile. 'I've never owned a house. It's quite a commitment.'

Jacinta shrugged. 'So you're a commitment-phobe. If you decide you don't want to live there you could rent it out. Property like that will appreciate in value. The rent will probably cover repayments. It's quite a reasonable price they're asking actually. It will go quickly.'

He risked another glance. 'You sound very savvy about the property market.'

She looked away, not willing to go into details about her paranoid need for security. A legacy from too many bills and not enough money with her mother. 'Isn't everyone nowadays?'

'I like the house,' he said slowly, as if just realizing how much. Then he grinned. 'I actually love the house and all the crazy bits that go with it. I just find it so sad that someone has put their whole life into creating their home and it can be bought by a passer-by as a packaged item.'

Now she understood. Shook her head. Some didn't get that chance. 'I don't see it like that. I admire a life well lived. The owner of that house had a full and interesting world, obviously different to that of your average man, and probably with philosophies a lot in common with yours. I think he'd be pleased to see someone like-minded adding their life experiences to his.'

The car slowed and Jonah looked at her. 'Where on earth do women come up with things like that?' He looked back at the street and shook his head. 'Don't get me wrong – I love the concept, but the guy is dead.'

Jacinta rolled her eyes. 'He lives on in his house.'

'Oh, great, there'll be two of us living there.'

Jacinta couldn't help the giggle that started way down in her stomach. She loved it. She loved the craziness of the conversation and being around Jonah made her feel alive. Hadn't she always been alive?

Jonah looked back at her. 'What do you think? Should I buy the house even though it's haunted?'

To heck with being restrained. 'Yes. I liked the turret room and it probably has secret passageways.'

Jonah started to laugh. 'I should have known you'd say that. But that proves it. The three of us think I should buy the house – and that includes the guy who haunts it.'

'If it's haunted, at least the house won't be lonely when you're away.'

She saw him bite back the grin. Laughing at her. This time she didn't mind.

Jonah nodded his head judiciously. 'So true. I was worried about that.'

Jacinta could contain her curiosity no longer. 'So tell me about where you've worked and how long you've been a foreign aid doctor.'

'I've been working for the medical arm of Missions Pacific for about ten years. My parents were missionary doctors before they died and I grew up in out-of-the-way villages in Papua New Guinea before my sister and I came to Australia for boarding school.' He shrugged. 'PNG was a little less politically interesting then, but if you're careful it's still a wonderful country.'

He turned into Jacinta's driveway and she decided it was worth the risk of more time spent with him. 'Would you like to come in for coffee?'

He looked at her and there was a twinkle in his eyes. 'I thought you were both going out.'

'We can go this afternoon.'

Twenty minutes later the three of them sat in the den, with Jacinta and Noni listening in fascination to Jonah's descriptions of remote villages, exotic wildlife and medical emergencies managed with the barest essentials.

Jacinta couldn't get enough. 'Is your sister still in PNG?'

'She died.' The words hung in the air as if he needed to remind himself as well as her. 'But, yes, she is buried over there.'

Jacinta paused, horrified at her blunder. 'I'm so sorry to hear that.' She frowned as something else he'd said at the hospital made more sense. 'Is her death why you said the country is too dangerous for families?'

'A lot to do with it, though the Papuans on the whole are a happy people.'

'Tell me about where you work. How big is the hospital?'

Jonah's eyes took on a far-away look. 'A hundred beds. Pudjip's not big but it's busy. We see four hundred inpatients and four thousand outpatients a month.' He smiled at the memories and then looked back at her, and she was glad to see his darkness had lifted.

'It's not just tropical diseases either. We do everything, and I mean everything. We have eighty to ninety obstetric deliveries and sixty to seventy major surgical procedures, as well as chemotherapy, pediatrics and health screening.'

Jacinta sighed. 'It sounds fascinating and adventurous, compared to what I do now.'

'Oh, it would be an adventure all right, Dr McCloud,' he mimicked her, 'but I think there are specific dangers for women.' His face was grim. 'Very specific.'

She lifted her chin. 'It still sounds amazing.'

He glared at her. 'It's stinking hot and primitive, and therefore unsanitary in a lot of the villages. And outside the compound rebel gangs are happy to kill.'

She returned his stare calmly. 'Do you think I'm too weak for PNG?'

Jacinta had baited him and he bit back. 'Not weak. Luscious.'

'Sexist.'

'Just looking for a way to make my point.'

She tipped her chin up. 'Good to see what strategies you're happy to use.'

Now they glared at each other.

Noni looked at them as each tried to stare the other down. 'Now, children. Play nicely.' She glanced at Jacinta as if to say, are you okay?

Jacinta stood up and Jonah did too. She held out her hand and smiled. 'Thank you for an interesting morning, Jonah.'

He smiled grimly and took her fingers in his. 'Thank you for coming with me to see the house. Goodbye, Jacinta.' He looked towards her stepmother. 'It was a pleasure to meet you, Noni.'

'You too, Jonah.'

Jacinta preceded him to the door and stood beside it to see him out. 'Good luck.' Silently she added, And I'll do what I want to do no matter what you say.

Jonah

Jonah walked down the path and slid into his hire car. It had been a disquieting morning.

There'd been dashes of delightful amusement as they bantered, and when he'd met Jacinta's eyes it was as if they'd known each other for years. He couldn't deny he was fiercely attracted to her and he didn't think she was immune to him. Kindling her interest in Papua New Guinea had been stupid.

Jonah frowned as he reversed out of the driveway.

All he could hope for was that she was dreaming, all talk and no action, but his instincts told him she was the wrong woman for that. He'd seen her eyes narrow and the speculative look she'd given him when he'd said Pudjip was no place for a woman.

Still, she had a good job that she couldn't possibly leave, so she was probably safe. Which was just as well, because she was a fascinating woman and the thought of her day in and day out at Pudjip unsettled him even thinking about it.

He'd love to know what made Jacinta McCloud tick. What was her background?

Jonah steered the car towards the estate agent's to discuss a house that he suddenly had to buy. He had no desire to look at any other property. As soon as the paperwork was organized and signed, he'd head back to work. It was too attractive around here for a single man with a job to do.

Jacinta

For Jacinta, an idea that had started as crazy soon became an obsession and she began to gather information on outreach medicine and Papua New Guinea.

During medical school, tropical medicine had always seemed particularly exotic to her.

Here was something she could sink her teeth into and meet her need for a change. Of course, her decision had very little to do with Jonah Armstrong, but she did think it strange the conversation she'd had with him never left her for long.

While she admitted he piqued her interest, the lure of Jonah was a fleeting thing. With her deep-seated distrust of relying on anyone, she doubted she would ever settle down with a man. She was her own woman and always would be.

Though she had to acknowledge that the possibility of a little more interaction with Jonah was a pleasant thought.

But it was the idea of adventure after twelve years of circumspection that was particularly attractive. Even a little danger wouldn't be out of place in her ordered life.

All she needed to know was how to get involved in medical aid work. If she worked overseas only one short term a year, she'd been told she could retain her senior position at Pickford while gaining tropical medicine experience they could use.

The day she had enough information to make an informed decision arrived and there was no doubt this was what she wanted. Jacinta switched on her computer and e-mailed the company address on Jonah's card. If Missions Pacific wouldn't have her there was always Medecins Sans Frontieres.

At the back of her mind she accepted she would be disappointed if she couldn't work with Jonah's organization.

Along with the e-mail to Missions Pacific she phoned home to Burra.

Her father answered the phone and she smiled at the warmth in his voice when he realized who it was. 'Hi, Dad.' She plunged straight in. 'I'm thinking of spending some time in Papua New Guinea for locum medical experience.'

She listened to the silence as her father processed her statement, and he didn't disappoint her with meaningless protestations.

'That sounds challenging.' The touch of resignation for her decisions meant he wasn't going to argue.

Jacinta smiled appreciatively into the phone. 'You always said I should travel.'

'I was thinking somewhere less unsettled, but I do hear the scenery is beautiful.' He paused again as if unsure about his next statement. 'I know how independent you are, but I have contacts in the Australian embassy in Port Moresby. Would you mind if I phoned them just to set up an emergency contact if you need it?'

Good old Dad. It would have been good to have him there when she'd been a kid, and she'd come to see he would have wanted that as well. If only he'd known she existed.

She thought about his offer. Having backup was always good. She knew how things could take a dive into the unexpected and this was an outpost. 'I shouldn't need them if I'm dealing with Missions Pacific but thanks, yes. Great idea.' She teased him. 'Plus it will make you feel better.'

'It would.'

'Fine.' She pictured her father, tall and handsome with a frown on his face as he tried not to tell her what to do. She'd inherited a lot of her father's control needs herself and she understood him.

'So, what's the attraction in Papua New Guinea?'

No reason not to be honest. 'I met a foreign aid doctor and his passion for the work he does made me realize I hadn't found my niche. This could be it. I want to make a difference.'

'You do make a difference, Jacinta.' There was pride in her father's voice and she felt the tears sting her eyes. She knew he found it hard that she didn't want to spend more time at Burra.

'A little difference. Maybe. But in a cushy way.'

'Yes,' he said. 'Running a busy emergency department ten hours a day and working in a youth center is way too cushy. Papua New Guinea should be free of cushiness.' The dryness in his voice was unmistakable. 'But I'm sure you have looked into it. We'll be here if you need us. Hang on.'

There was a background conversation and her father laughed. 'Noni said to say hello to Jonah for her and she'll ring you tomorrow.'

Jacinta rang off, shook her head at her stepmother's cheekiness, and then sat back and waited to find out if she had a job.

Self-funding meant there was no problem setting her time limit and Jacinta planned on a four-week period to start with. It would be the adventure of a lifetime.

The next day Missions Pacific replied that they were willing to accept her offer and Jacinta asked for placement near Jonah if possible. It seemed crazy not to go for at least the region where she knew someone from the organization, and it didn't necessarily mean they would work together. Did it?

The next week was a flurry of clothes-hunting, house-sorting and a quick trip halfway to down the south coast of New South Wales towards Burra to meet Noni for lunch and the transfer of Moggy into Noni's car.

'Your father will get used to having a cat,' Noni reassured Jacinta, and they both laughed. 'Have you heard from Jonah?'

'I e-mailed him but he hasn't replied. He's possibly on a field trip or the phone lines could be down. Apparently, both are pretty common.'

Noni nodded and hugged her. 'Be careful. And as for Jonah, go with what feels right,' she said, and Jacinta kissed her goodbye.

The next day, the Port Moresby humidity hit Jacinta's face like a hot damp towel as soon as she poked her head out of the air-conditioned plane, but February was the end of summer so maybe it would get cooler.

The heat and bombardment of aromas were overwhelming. The scent of bougainvillea, the heavy sweetness of what she later found out to be the betel-nut chewed by the locals, the overlying cloying smell of rotting vegetation and good old-fashioned sweat all vied for her attention.

Strangely it was the brightness of the light and the vivid reds in the clothes of the native Papuans that caught her imagination.

Bright green vegetation around the airport made everything else look ordinary, even the aircraft, as she stepped down onto the steaming tarmac.

When she entered the terminal, huge rotating ceiling fans circulated the crowded bouquet of pungent aromas and she could feel the excitement in her blood almost fizzing and the smile on her face stretched.

'Dr McCloud?' Jacinta nodded at a grinning porter dressed in white. He waved the sign with her name on it. 'I'm Jimmy Puk Puk from the mission. I'll take you across to the MAF plane.' He had the brightest set of white teeth she'd ever seen, and Jacinta grinned back.

MAF Plane? Ah, Missionary Air Fellowship plane. Jointly owned by all the missions.

Dressed in shorts and shirt, Jimmy's feet were dustily bare and he held out his left hand to take her bag. Her eyes were drawn to the healed stump where his right hand should have been.

He caught her glance and grinned again. "That's why they call me Jimmy Puk Puk. Puk Puk mean croc, 'cos I took more than his hand when I caught up with that puk puk.'

Jimmy directed her off to a side aisle and broke into a melodic Pidgin English discussion with the customs officer until they were waved through to another gateway and back onto the tarmac.

Jacinta had been studying the Papuan Pidgin English at home for the last week, along with a brush-up on tropical illnesses, and she'd followed a little of the discussion. It was daunting how much she couldn't understand. Hopefully when a sick Papuan was trying to tell her where it hurt, she'd be able to get the gist.

Out in the sunlight, Jimmy switched back to English to direct her into a beaten-up open Jeep and helped her climb in.

'Mission car,' he said briefly, and Jacinta wondered if he meant he wouldn't own a bomb like this or he didn't own a car at all. 'We go to other side of airport so you can fly to Mt Hagen.'

Missions Pacific was based east of Mt Hagen at the hillside village hospital at Pudjip, high in the mountains. At least away from the coast malaria was less of a problem, though that hadn't helped Jonah she reminded herself.

When she arrived in Mt Hagen, she'd meet the experienced preceptor who would ultimately be responsible for settling her into the corps, and she hoped he spoke English.

Jimmy drove like a maniac and her fingers whitened on the edge of the door, which she clung to. Macabre images of a long rectangular box containing her corpse being slowly carried off the plane to the accompaniment of drumbeats at Sydney airport made Jacinta shudder and realize how far she was from home and the usual safety of her environment.

How the heck had she arrived at this point? Just why was she here? Jacinta swallowed a half-hysterical laugh as Jimmy almost rolled the vehicle to miss a dog that flew at them from under an old truck and diverted herself with her reasons.

She'd always been interested in tropical medicine.

Jonah had painted a picture that had called to her sense of adventure, though he'd tried hard to convince her otherwise. The thought made her wonder again if attempting this trip was a knee-jerk reaction to Jonah telling her she couldn't do it.

Before she could get too bogged down in self-recriminations they swerved back towards a very much smaller red and white aircraft parked under a tree.

It was such a shame Jimmy ran over the edge of a basket of chickens as he braked.

Amidst the terrified squawks and flying feathers, vitriolic abuse flew at Jimmy – and to a lesser extent Jacinta – from a wizened old woman with a red-stained toothless mouth who sprang out from under the wing of the aircraft to gather her escaping livestock.

'Kakuruk bugga up,' she screamed.

Jimmy just laughed. 'She say the chook no good now.'

Jacinta climbed shakily out of the Jeep and brushed herself down. One chicken would never lay again and the old lady clucked and hung it from her belt by a thong. Jacinta had a fair idea what would be eaten in the woman's house tonight.

Life was certainly different here.

A dour middle-aged man appeared from the back of the plane and wiped his fingers on his trousers before offering his hand to Jacinta.

'You'll be the doctor for Hagen, then?' His thick Scottish brogue sounded strange in this steaming environment.

She nodded. 'Jacinta McCloud. Have you been waiting for me?'

'Aye. And I'll be glad to get off the ground before the breeze picks up any more. This way, Doctor.'

He took her soft carry on and compact bag and squeezed them in behind the seat then reached down and threw the chicken basket on top of it.

'In you get, Mimi,' he said to the old woman who climbed reluctantly into the back of the aircraft first. 'Mimi had surgery and is flying home with us today.'

Jacinta nodded and smiled at the older lady, who apparently still harbored a grudge about the loss of her chicken and stared inscrutably back.

Great, Jacinta winced. I've made my first enemy.

She followed Mimi into the back and waved to Jimmy Puk Puk who smiled cheerfully as he returned to his Jeep.

'Mr. McTash very experienced pilot.' Jimmy called out with a big grin. 'You crash, he very experienced. Had many, many crash landing.'

Jacinta stared at Jimmy through the window as the pilot shut her in, and her last sight of Jimmy was of the little man rolling around in his seat, laughing. Too much information, Jacinta thought grimly.

When they were safely in the air, she leaned forward towards the pilot to make herself heard. 'Does it take long to get to Mt Hagen?'

'Long way lik lik, as they say,' he said with almost a smile. 'That means it's not "close to" and it's not "long way more, more yet".'

Terrific. The guy was a mine of information. Jacinta nodded as if she understood, smiled and then leaned back in her seat and closed her eyes. She should have spent more time on the phrase book.

The flight to Mt Hagen hid the view thanks to the low clouds, with the occasional mountain range or river visible below in glimpses. Mostly uneventful except for the panic of Mimi every time the aircraft flew into the slightest turbulence. When Mimi screamed, Jacinta's heart rate doubled, the panicked chickens would set up a squawk in caged agitation and the aircraft would bump along with the exhausting in-flight diversion.

Finally, Jacinta took Mimi's hand in hers and squeezed it. 'Don't worry, Mimi,' she said. 'We'll be there soon.' Though she wasn't sure if she was reassuring the old woman or herself. Either way, the woman seemed to settle a little with Jacinta's reassurance.

By the time the plane made its approach to what appeared to Jacinta as an extremely short landing strip on top of a ridge, she was longing to throw herself on the ground and kiss the moist earth herself.

It had been a long day.

When she dragged her carry-on across the paddock towards the arrival hall a little later, she hoped the next "Jimmy" would give her a more relaxing ride.

Despite the clouds, the air remained atrociously hot, although not as steamy as Port Moresby, and she lifted the neck of her shirt away from her skin to let in some of the warm breeze.

Her step faltered as she recognized the familiar figure in the shade of the building and she finally admitted how much she had relied on the chance Jonah would meet her.

He was much taller and sturdier than the native Papuans she'd seen so far, and she was very glad to see him in this unfamiliar environment. She thought he still looked slightly jaundiced but that could have been related to the lack of warmth in his eyes. There was no sign of weakness as he reached over and took her case, lifting it as easily as if it were filled with cotton balls. He stared down into her face for a moment and she couldn't read his expression. She waited for a smile that didn't come and her stomach sank with disappointment.

'It's a small world, Dr McCloud,' he drawled sardonically, and she realized he was definitely not pleased to see her.

'Too small for both of us, Dr Armstrong?'

'The whims of the well-heeled are strange. Hope you can cope with the lack of amenities,' he said, and Jacinta thought briefly of the squalor she'd lived in after her mother had died. Before her father had come for her.

'I think I'll manage.'

Jonah

Jonah watched Jacinta lift her chin at his comment and fought against softening this attitude towards her. He ran his free hand – the one not lugging her compact suitcase – over his head.

This was a bad sign. He'd started the week furious when he'd discovered the identity of the new doctor, and had worked his way through the fury with cold, logical planning on how to make her go home.

He'd considered and discarded several plans that included appealing to her good sense, horrifying her with reality, frightening her with facts, or wearing her down with a heavy workload.

Then he'd arrived at the more basic idea of just plain carrying her back onto the aircraft she got off. Though, from the little he'd seen of Jacinta, he really didn't think any of the options would work.

He tried to regain some of his decisiveness and glanced down at her as she skipped beside him, trying to keep up. She was frowning and those heavy brows of hers signaled her displeasure as if she'd hoisted a flag. And, Lord help him, that frown made him smile.

The smile faded when he realized the depth of his dilemma. He hadn't wanted her to come but now he couldn't wish her gone. It felt too good just to look at her.

'I'd planned on sending you back as soon as possible,' he growled. 'Unfortunately, my assistant came down with what I suspect is the same kind of malaria I succumbed to, and I've had to ship him out. We'll all have to carry the slack of one man down for a while. You'll stay your term and that includes the Sepik trip I've promised to join.' He glanced across at her. 'If you're on Doxycycline you'll have to change your antimalarial as they have a resistant strain down there that's knocking them down like flies. Though where you'll be for the next week or two isn't so bad.'

The thought of Jacinta as sick as James filled Jonah's gut with cold dread because he knew how powerless they could be to protect her from disease. He'd just have to be vigilant.

He shook her bag. 'I hope you've got your repellent and long-sleeved shirts in this bag. If I catch you after sunset in short sleeves, I'll personally dress you.'

He saw the disappointment cross her face. That's right. I am not pleased to see you here. Pleased to see you, yes, but not HERE. Cold dread settled in Jonah's stomach when he thought about the last time he'd seen his sister alive. Confident and airily brushing off the dangers. Look where that had ended. Now Jacinta. He wouldn't let that happen. She had to go back.

If she ended up thinking he'd never liked her, well that was a good thing.

'Quite the little demigod on your home turf, Dr Armstrong.' Her tone was saccharine sweet.

'Responsibility does that to people up here. I hate sending people home in pine boxes.' He saw her wince. Hopefully she was considering that Jonah hadn't exaggerated the risks quite as much as she'd thought.

He started the vehicle and they left the airport in silence. After about ten minutes she said, 'At least you drive considerably better than my last driver.'

Contrarily Jonah pressed harder on the pedal. 'It takes two hours to travel to our destination and hopefully we won't have any issues before we get there.'

After that very little was said between them.

By the time they pulled up at the Pudjip Station gates a little before sunset, apparently his passenger had decided two could play at being distant. He glanced at the sun and pointedly at her bare arms. He hoped that the next chance she had she'd slip her long-sleeved shirt on rather than have to act on his threat.

He regretted being quite so over the top with the grumpiness but she didn't have to know that.

Wordlessly she followed him around the side of the hospital to the huts beyond. Her hut had many louvred windows, all screened, and inside lay plain furnishings and a lockable door. There was a narrow single bed with a mosquito net suspended above it. A thin sheet and blanket lay folded on the bed. An old school desk and chair offered a workplace.

'You have the en-suite.' Jonah pointed to the bowl and jug of water for washing. 'Ladies' toilet is also the men's room and is around the corner next to the laundry. Knock firmly before you enter and if it's empty lock the door when you're in there. Try not to go at night.'

'I'm sure I'll manage.' She tilted her head. 'What makes it less dangerous here for you than for me, apart from the fact that I'm a woman?'

See. No idea. He wanted to hit the wall he was so terrified for her and that in itself wasn't useful at all. 'You mean apart from my time as a surgeon in the army? Or the fact that I grew up here? Or the fact that the boys don't fancy me?' Sarcasm dripped. 'Gee, Dr McCloud, I guess there's no reason I should be safer than you.'

He wondered how long before he recovered from her arrival. Jacinta compressed her lips and just nodded politely as he spoke.

'Silly question.'

Great. Now he was in the wrong. 'That's right. I'll meet you at the top of the steps of the hospital in ten minutes if you'd like to wash and...' he glanced at her bare arms '...change.'

He saw the narrowing of her eyes but she didn't bite. Full marks to her. She could keep her temper and he admired her even more for that seeing as how he was behaving like an arrogant beast.

He sighed. He guessed she wasn't going to quit in a hurry.

Jacinta

Exactly ten minutes later Jacinta stood outside the single-storied hospital's front entrance with her arms safely covered in a long-sleeved shirt and suitably plastered with repellent.

Jonah was waiting. Since her arrival she hadn't caught even a glimpse of the warm and delightful man who'd made her laugh that day in Bondi. Jonah towered over her with a grim visage. His implacability made him seem even larger than she remembered.

In fact, he was insufferable. Not one welcoming word and his blue eyes were icy with hostility. She didn't recall any indication he was a closet dictator in Sydney.

Well, she was darned if she was going to let him know he'd disappointed her.

At least no smart comment on her obedient sleeves, thankfully.

'I'll take you in and introduce you around.'

They moved through the doors and she glanced up at the slowly rotating ceiling fans, surprised how cool it was inside the building as they walked across to a plain wooden desk at the head of the room that served as the nurse's desk. The woman seated there had by far the darkest skin Jacinta had seen and her dark coiled hair was piled high on her head with a bone clasp.

'Dr Jacinta McCloud, this is Carla. Carla is the head nurse and will help you with your clinics.'

Carla smiled shyly. Thank goodness. Finally, a friendly face.

'Welcome, Doctor.'

'Thank you.' Jacinta slanted a look at Jonah. See, arrogant man. That's how it's done. Jacinta held out her hand and took the woman's capable fingers. 'It's nice to meet you, Carla.' They shook and Carla came around from behind the desk to accompany them.

They moved down the room in a trio.

A teenage boy hurried in through a side door carrying a jug of water and Jonah stopped him. 'This is Jay. He's our orderly, or, as they call them here, doctor boy.'

'Hello, Jay.' Jacinta smiled and the boy ducked his head shyly, the black springy coils of his hair gleaming in the fluorescent light.

They moved on.

A tall, blond-haired man in theatre scrubs bounded up the side steps and stopped beside them.

Jonah gestured with his hand. 'Dr Jacinta McCloud, this tall streak of American dynamism is Dr Chuck Ford. Chuck's been here four months and goes home next month. He can't get enough of us.'

Chuck grinned and held out his hand. 'Hi there, Jacinta. Welcome to Pudjip. It's a wild place.' He looked at Jonah. 'We've an early mark in Theatre today so I'm off to delivery to see what I can see.'

'Don't you love the enthusiasm of youth?' Jonah's comment was more under his breath than out loud, but Jacinta heard it and stored his cynicism to ponder later. She hadn't picked that in Sydney. Had something happened? Before she could wonder more, he turned back to her.

'The first week you'll practice the language working here in Pud-jip while you conduct physical examinations, take histories and note symptoms. Most of it will be in Pidgin English. Once you're more confident with the language it will be a lot easier for you.' He glanced around. 'The difficult thing to accept is that the choices for treatment at home are not obtainable here. You have to learn what's available and what's not for your treatment options. Carla will help you there. After that orientation you'll go on call here for a week to get some skills in treating the illnesses that are most common.' He paused. Glanced briefly at her face.

She nodded that she understood and he went on.

'If you handle that, you can accompany me on the next mission trip. Those trips last about ten days and we take a medical team to an outreach health center. I gather your term is four weeks?'

He shot her a look and Jacinta returned it calmly. 'Does that mean we're together for the next month?'

When he nodded with another one of those sardonic smiles, she was careful to keep her face expressionless.

Great, she thought, attitude for weeks. But she'd asked for it. She'd go to a different place next time. Jacinta glanced down the rows of mostly full beds. Then at Carla. 'So, how many patients have you in at the moment?'

If he was disappointed that she didn't comment on them being together for an extended time, he didn't show it. He answered for Carla. 'About eighty, but we had more than a hundred here during the chickenpox epidemic last year.'

One of the patients called out to the nurse and she left the two doctors to complete the tour on their own.

'I hope I don't see an epidemic while I'm here,' Jacinta said.

'So do I,' he said soberly. 'We lose too many patients and the children break your heart.'

Stricken, she stared at him, and at her distress he finally eased up on her. He ran his hand over the back of his head. 'Hang it, Jacinta, why did you come?'

'Because I can help?' she suggested quietly.

He rubbed his head again and she wondered if he had a headache. Probably from stewing over her arrival. The thought made her smile. So he was a grump, not a dictator, and she could forgive him that.

She went on. 'Because I'm interested in tropical medicine and always have been. Because I do have something to offer and the time and money to spare to make it happen. Do you have the resources to turn that kind of help away?' This was the crux of the matter.

His sigh came from the depths of his being. 'No, I don't. We do need people like you and I guess you'll come to realize that this place is more than some big adventure. I just, personally, wish you hadn't come.'

'Gee, thanks. That was the impression I got at the airstrip.'

He laughed without amusement. 'Impressions can be deceptive. If I was in Sydney I'd be delighted to see you. You're not hard on the eye.'

She suppressed her smile. Good grief. 'Was that a backhanded compliment, Dr Armstrong? I may faint.'

'No fainting until your days off, Doctor.' But this time he smiled.

Jonah drank in the sight of her. He couldn't help himself. It wasn't his problem if she decided she could handle this place and take care of herself. But if anything happened to her, he knew it would be his concern no matter what she or he said, and that terrified him.

Her tailored trousers and long-sleeved top were loose enough to keep her cool but fitted enough to let him know there was a very desirable woman under those clothes. And that was the meat of the problem. He found her very desirable.

She'd probably bought her clothes through some yuppie traveler's mail-order site because, though they were appropriate, they just shrieked money and style. The whims of the rich. He hoped no miscreant decided she was worth a good ransom.

How she would cope with the primitive conditions was yet to be seen, but he had to admit she hadn't commented on anything so far as being unsatisfactory.

Her dark hair was confined in a tight bun to keep her cool in the heat, but it left the lovely curve of her neck so softly vulnerable he wanted to put a scarf on her. And the way she kept raising those extraordinary brows at him every time he barked at her, he was hard put not to smile.

He'd have to be extra careful he didn't get used to having her around because she was only here for a short time.

On the good side, it could prove to be an interesting month, as long as he could keep her safe from the dangers in PNG and the bigger danger of himself.

He watched her over the next few days and he could tell the experience was unlike anything Jacinta had expected.

She obviously struggled with the language, every new recruit was the same, the dialects of the visiting sick kept changing and it was slow going, learning Pidgin English. But she persevered. Her clinical skills delighted him.

By the fifth day he suspected she could pick up most of the important information her patients wanted to convey to her, but there were healthy doses of hand motions included.

She called him after a particularly frustrating half-hour trying to understand an elderly woman with abdominal pain. Jonah asked the question and in one short sharp sentence he discovered the woman thought she'd swallowed a chicken bone that she could feel in her stomach.

Jacinta sighed. 'I can't believe that was what she was trying to say.'

She had no idea how advanced she'd become in such a short time. 'You have to understand that English is spoken by only one to two per cent of the inhabitants. Pidgin is widespread but there are seven hundred and fifteen indigenous languages to mix with it. You can imagine the struggle for the ruling government to be understood by even half the people.'

'Seven hundred and fifteen? You're kidding me.'

'Probably more.'

'Then I don't feel so bad.'

'You're doing remarkably well.'

'Now I think I'm going to faint. Praise again?' She pretended to take a photo with an imaginary camera. 'I'll hug that grain to pull out later tonight.'

Then she turned and concentrated on her patient.

Jacinta

The next night, after another frantic clinical day complete, the medical staff had met and eaten supper and the lights were being extinguished all over the station.

Jacinta leaned on the doorframe of her room and pondered how in some ways the hospital wasn't as primitive as she'd feared.

There was a telephone and Jonah had set up an internet account for her, so she could at least e-mail Noni and her father when the phone lines were working, which they sometimes did.

In other ways it was more primitive than she had ever imagined. To the PNG nationals, death by illness and violence and accident were sad facts of life, and the lack of medical supplies ensured that she would never take for granted her facilities in Sydney.

To Jacinta's surprise she felt a kinship with the people she'd met. She delighted in the shy smiles and singing as the women worked, the happy children – both PNG nationals and missionary kids – who played so well together, and the bright clothes worn by the locals.

And she wept inside for the stoic acceptance when illnesses that had brought patients to the mission hospital had taken too great a hold to be cured.

'You shouldn't be outside in the dark!'

Jonah's voice made her heart trip and she snapped her head around. In trouble again. 'I didn't hear you come across the gravel.'

'I'm an elephant compared to some of the locals,' he growled, 'which is why you shouldn't be out here alone after dark. You should stay locked in your room.'

Jonah looked genuinely upset and in the few days she'd been there she'd heard enough gruesome stories to accept he was only concerned for her safety. But she hated being in the wrong.

'I'm sorry.' She stepped back into her doorway. 'You're right, but it was such a beautiful night after this afternoon's rain. I needed to feel the air. Are you going for a walk?'

Jacinta could hear the wistfulness in her own voice and she suspected he did, too, because he sighed.

'Only a short one, but you can come if you wish.'

His tone wasn't as welcoming as she'd have liked but the lure of some time outside the hut was too attractive to be picky. She slipped back inside to grab her light cardigan and on her return was surprised when he took her hand as they began to walk. His hand was cool, despite the heat, and firmly held her fingers.

She blinked. 'Hadn't expected that.'

He looked down at their entwined fingers, a hold that should have felt companionable and safe. But didn't. 'This is just to stop you wandering off. At least I have some control over the danger, if I can pull you back out of the way.' There was a tiny hint of amusement in his voice and she could feel the spread of euphoria that they were regaining some of the banter she remembered from Sydney.

'And I thought you just wanted to hold my hand.'

'That, too,' he said, as if them doing so was the most natural thing in the world.

She was plunged back into confusion.

It terrified her the way he could rouse her emotions with a touch and then dash her down with a curt reprimand. Was he aware of what he did to her or was it just her that was supersensitive?

'Why?'

'I told you. To save you from predators.'

Jacinta could feel the pull of attraction and the frivolous conversation belied the depth of tension slowly building to fog between them. The scent of soap from his shower drifted towards her every now and then as they walked, and the almost silent tread of his footsteps – so much quieter than hers, as if he'd learnt to walk silently for a reason – made her aware of his powerful frame, always leashed but ready in an instant to glide into action.

He laughed and she closed her eyes briefly at the warmth in that sound.

'You are such a prickly woman,' he murmured.

'Spare me. You're a cranky bear half the time. Probably more.' Jacinta exhaled noisily. 'You confuse me and I find that hard to cope with.'

'Honest Jacinta.'

His comment made her feel uncomfortable because there was so much he didn't know about her. So much she held tight inside. Did that constitute dishonesty or was she allowed that self-protection?

She changed the subject. Asked a question she often thought of at night and never had time for in the day. 'Did you buy the house in Bondi that we looked at?'

He laughed, a deep gust of heat in the night. 'Yes, I did. My solicitor e-mailed me yesterday to say the sale was through. So, I now have my first official home in Australia.'

He officially owned a residence a street away from her. 'Are you glad?' She had to admit she was.

He shrugged and she suspected he still hovered, ambivalent about proprietorship. 'It feels strange to be a home owner. Maybe I'm growing up.'

She laughed at that, and nudged his arm with her shoulder as they walked. 'Don't grow much more or you won't fit through the doorway of your new home.'

His voice lowered teasingly. 'Does it bother you?'

Jacinta wasn't sure what he was asking. Did she mind that his home was in her 'hood? Did she mind that he was the approximate size of a man-mountain? Did she mind that the teasing depth of his voice turned her insides into mush?

Had he been feeling the same build-up of tension, the same link from her hands to her libido she was? He had to be. She had to know.

'What are you asking, Jonah? Am I bothered that we're holding hands and ignoring the obvious?'

'The obvious...?'

'I don't know what you call it, but I'd say attraction.'

The word seemed to echo in the night air and reverberate through her body. What if he knocked her back? That would be awkward. She couldn't bear the tension, the sense of not knowing where she stood with this irascible man.

'Why don't you kiss me and we'll see if I'm right.'

He paused. Looked down at her and she saw his surprise. Even admiration. When he tightened his grip and tugged her to face him, she felt the satisfaction of being brave and being rewarded. 'I don't mind if I do,' he said, and his other hand came up and cupped her face to cradle her cheek.

Then their lips touched gently and with the first warmth of his breath, hers caught. His mouth brushed hers, and his hands slid down to pull her closer against him. Her freed hand slid up and over the muscles bunched beneath his shirt, and she slid her savoring fingers onto his shoulders and neck with a sigh as the kiss deepened.

'Mmhm.' As amazing as she'd thought it would be to kiss Jonah.

'Mmhm what?' he murmured against her mouth. Nipping at her lip.

She sighed into him, too delighted to talk, and they both forgot the past and slid headlong into the present.

Jonah

For Jonah, kissing Jacinta encapsulated everything he'd feared. He suppressed a groan at the sweetness she offered him, but in his heart he'd known it would be like this. He'd known from the first moment he'd opened his eyes at Pickford that she would be a danger to everything he thought he had control over.

The kiss waxed and waned and expanded again, and his stomach kicked with every stroke of his tongue against hers. Every nuance of movement burned like a furnace against him and he could feel the control slipping from his fingers like silk through a golden keyhole.

They had to stop.

He had to stop because she – the temptress who'd provoked him into this – wasn't going to.

Slowly he pulled back, lowered her feet to the ground and released her. She swayed slightly in his arms as if she would fall and his grip tightened until she steadied. Then, as much as he didn't want to, he put her away from him.

'Your height doesn't bother me.' Her voice drifted towards him, still a little dreamy and he couldn't suppress a smile.

He peered at her face in the moonlight and fought against his fierce desire to pull her back into his arms. He had no idea what she was talking about.

His mind fogged with that overpowering urge to just pick her up and carry her back to his hut. That – and all the reasons he couldn't – made thinking sensibly almost impossible. He struggled to find something to say. Anything to break the silence and the spell.

'I admire the way you've coped with our primitive conditions.'

She straightened and pulled her hand free to put more distance between them. Peered at him as she brushed her hair out of her eyes. 'What?'

What had he been saying? Ah yes. 'You've tried hard. Fitted in really well here, especially when you're used to the high life.' He didn't know why he'd added that last part because he didn't know that. Then again, any life in Sydney would be high life compared to here.

She stared at him. 'Don't patronize me, Jonah. You know nothing of my life, so don't prejudge through ignorance.'

Jonah stopped. Played what he'd said back and winced. Yep, patronizing. To make Director of a city ED at her age, he knew how hard she must have worked.

And that was all he knew about her.

Just what he'd seen in Sydney.

The daughter of doctor, a doting stepmother and a substantial flat in a premium beach suburb. He'd used those scant facts to paint a picture of privilege and that was patently unfair.

He'd upset her and it was a measure of the imbalance she caused him that he'd done so. Maybe it was better to re-establish some distance between them. 'I apologize.' He cast a brief look towards the stars for inspiration – for words that would not compound his mistake. 'So, why don't you tell me, Jacinta? Why do you manage so well?'

She looked up at him and lowered her brows, and he realized she was trying to judge his sincerity. Had he been that hard on her? Well, yes. To protect himself and that had been selfish. She had the right to glare, probably. And kissing her had been a poor choice. 'I'm serious. I'd like to know.'

They started to walk again and he took back her hand. After some initial resistance, she let him, and the measure of his relief increased in direct proportion to his trepidation for the future. The warmth of her fingers in his did strange things to his heart and he nearly missed her next words.

'My mother was a single parent and we were dirt poor. Poor as in second-hand – probably third-hand – clothes and watery vegetable soups. That level of poverty. We only scraped through as well as we did because she refused to be beaten. I admired her greatly.'

'It must have been hard for you.'

'It was harder for her, and I'll never know why she chose not to tell my father of my existence, because I've come to believe he would have eased that burden.'

Jacinta's voice came out of the dimness beside him spoke of dark times and a feeling of vulnerability he wished he could have helped with. But it also spoke of a woman who didn't want that help.

'What happened to your mother?'

'She died in childbirth, from a congenital heart condition. I ran away from the man she lived with and ended up in Kings Cross in squatters' digs and conditions that weren't much different to these.' She lifted her hand to include the camp. 'And in some ways much worse than here.'

He couldn't visualize this stylish, fiercely intelligent woman as a grieving, lost street teen. 'How old were you?'

'Sixteen.'

He shuddered and tried not to imagine what it must have been like for her.

Her voice dropped and he had to strain to catch her next words. 'I fell pregnant, and when the man who'd used me threw me out, I moved in with some drug dealing drag queens. I ironed their costumes. They were kind and I'm excellent with an iron.'

He swallowed and kept his voice light. 'I'll remember that. Though not a lot of call for that in the bush here in PNG.'

'You never know,' she said. 'Then a bloke arrived from out of nowhere and said he was my dad. That he'd tracked me down from a lost letter my mother had finally sent. He took me in for the last two months of my pregnancy and looked after me.'

'So you'd been managing for yourself for almost a year before your dad found you?'

A lot could happen, and probably had happened, in that year. She would have had to rely on her own wits to survive. He'd said she was used to the high-life. He wanted to kick himself. Hard. 'It must have been strange to meet him. I gather you knew nothing about him?'

'Strange is a good description,' she said with a tight little laugh. 'I had no idea he existed and then... there he was. So kind and patient, while he was learning too, and wanting to make up for all those years. But he was a stranger. A complete and utter stranger. If I hadn't been pregnant and scared for my unborn baby I wouldn't have gone. It took me a long time to trust that he was part of my life. That he wouldn't decide that he didn't want me again.'

Jonah tightened his grip on her hand in support. In comfort. He had no words.

She shrugged. 'That was what I'd learnt up till then. Men would let you down if you relied on them. Better to make do, and not wait for the time they would let you down.' There was the hint of a smile in her voice when she spoke again. 'Iain was very patient with the surly teenager I was. He supported me when things were tough until I could stand on my own two feet. Noni and Dad were there for me...' Her voice dropped even further, to a hoarse whisper. 'When my baby died.'

He felt as if someone had grabbed his chest and squeezed it, hard, and he realized that he who dealt with death and illness every day could scarcely bear the thought of Jacinta's suffering. 'I'm so sorry to hear of your loss. How did your baby die?'

She lifted her chin. 'Same as my mum. She was four weeks old when she began to show symptoms, but she touched all our lives with tiny fingers and the biggest determination to live, it's her strength that I'll never forget.'

He could only imagine the pain such a loss would cause to a mother. All he could go on was what he saw in his work as a doctor and the feelings he'd been left with after his sister, Melinda, had died.

He wanted to hug Jacinta close in sympathy – to take her pain and protect her from ever feeling such agony again. But he could no more protect her from that than he could promise to keep her safe here. Which was why he wanted her to leave. Why he needed her gone.

Then she asked for his torch.

He'd carried it but they hadn't used it. He handed it to her and she stopped and turned her ankle. The light beam illuminated the slim curve of her lower leg and he looked down to see what she was pointing to.

'This is my butterfly.' There was a tiny pink and green winged figure tattooed on her ankle. He wasn't a fan of tattoos, but this one touched him in a way he didn't understand. She switched the torch off and the darkness closed around them as his eyes tried to adjust to the sudden loss of light.

Her voice carried softly. 'In memory of my daughter, Olivia – just like your butterfly...' she touched the ring on his finger '...your own butterfly in memory of your sister. We do have something in common.'

His gut twisted. They had too much in common. Grief and loss and the horror from when Melinda disappeared settled over him like a dank fog, and he wished uselessly and with all his heart that Jacinta were safely back in Sydney.

He also wished she hadn't told him about her daughter because now he felt even closer to her.

They'd both been shaped by tragedy in their past and he didn't doubt that she was stronger from the loss of her daughter. He could feel himself drawn more and more under her spell every second, and that wasn't good.

At work, settled into routine, she meshed so seamlessly with the ethos of the hospital. His personal misgivings had struggled under the weight of relief to have another doctor, and a fabulous one at that, on board. The challenge of maintaining his distance from her was undermining his good intentions. His admiration of how well she coped with the workload and the environment was part of it, but the fact that he was so aware of her sensual presence unsettled him no matter what she was doing.

Any moment of the day, he could pick Jacinta's quiet voice out above others and recognize her soft laughter in a room full of people. Catch the scent of her shampoo as she passed. Sense her mood.

Even now, the cadence of her voice coming from the darkness beside him as they walked reminded him of his first memories of her during his delirium. And made him long to do all the things sleep allowed him to dream of at night alone in his bed.

Too many conflicting thoughts.

'Let's stop talking and listen to the night.' His voice was very quiet and deep. He turned his face up to the stars.

They were both silent for a few minutes, but the jungle around them rustled and croaked and shifted between the calls of night birds. The trees overhead creaked and shimmered in the moonlight castling deep shadows blacker than mere darkness. 'This is what I miss in the cities – the sounds and feel of the night.'

Jacinta

Jacinta could admit she didn't understand him.

What were his thoughts and the nuances behind the conflicting messages he telegraphed? Mostly she wondered why she'd told him more than she'd told anyone except her father and Noni.

This walk had brought too many thoughts and unanswered questions, so she too, concentrated on listening to the constant buzz and hum and tick of the insects and frogs.

Alone, she would have been uneasy with the rustle of undergrowth from the unseen animals and the call of some raucous bird, but with Jonah beside her it all combined to create an orchestra of living but invisible inhabitants of the bush.

As she savored how alive the night was, the moon shone down on the leaves of a soaring palm and clouds skittered behind the pointed leaves, dimming and then brightening their path.

'It's beautiful,' she sighed. His hand tightened on hers.

He didn't say anything for a few minutes and then he said, 'Yes, it is.' Then he sighed. 'Beautiful and dangerous.' He dropped her fingers and she felt suddenly rudderless in the dark. 'And so are you. That's what frightens me.' The ring on his finger glinted as he raised his hand to run his fingers through his hair.

When he started again, the stern inflection from Mt Hagen airport was back in his voice. 'Please, remember that it is not recommended for women to walk in the station at night on their own or walk off the station outside the gates at any time.'

She wished he'd let it rest. 'I hear you. But you are laboring the point.'

And spoiling the mood, she wanted to add.

Then he totally destroyed it. 'My sister never returned. Not alive. She broke the rule and paid the ultimate price.' With ultimate finality he said, 'I won't have that to happen to you.'

The next morning as the sun rose, as if to underscore his words of the night before, a young native woman was carried in on a makeshift stretcher by grieving relatives. Abducted by the rebel men, she'd suffered horrific burns and had been near death when her family had found her.

Jonah and Carla helped bandage the victim and give intravenous fluids, even though they knew they couldn't save her. At least morphine could lighten her pain.

When the young woman passed away just before lunchtime, Jacinta could feel the splintering of horror inside herself and the black ball of revenge lodged in her chest as she wished she could find those responsible.

'Don't go there, Jacinta.' Jonah had come up behind her.

She stood rigid on the back veranda of the hospital and her fingernails dug into a post in helpless rage. She shuddered when his fingers traced the tears down her cheek and he shook his head as he pulled her into his chest for comfort.

Then his arms came around her and she began to sob.

He allowed her to do so for a few moments and he stroked her hair before he spoke. 'They are not of your world. Rebel crime may have decreased in recent years but there's isolated instances and they can be horrific.

'You have to hang onto the fact that if people do horrid deeds, like today, then their own laws will catch up with them. There is darkness here but there is also the most beautiful spirit within these people.'

She lifted her eyes to his. 'You really believe that the beauty outweighs the bad?'

He shrugged. 'I have to. Because what we do matters, and I'm not willing to walk away from the good because of the bad.'

She sniffed and drew in a shaking breath as she dried her eyes on her sleeve. 'Their behavior puts a different light on my adventure.'

He smiled and hugged her close once more before he let her go. 'Is this where I get to tell you I told you so?'

She stiffened and he smiled again before he went on.

'Your heart's in the right place. Here, you learn to grow up fast.' He waved his hand at the ward adjacent to them. 'On bad days I feel so bent over with the weight of what I can't do I forget what we are achieving, and that is when I begin to straighten again.

'Things have greatly improved since the civil war ended. But I grew up with this life – I can't imagine how challenging it would be for someone from a different life to watch helplessly as things like this happen.

'A wise man said of our work, "We are hard-pressed but nowhere near hopeless".' He turned her around and pointed her towards the door of the hospital. 'I remember that when I feel like you do now.' He gave her a little push. 'You need to put an IV cannula in little Peeta. His chemotherapy is due and he doesn't cry when you do it. Then we must make the round of patients we didn't have time for this morning.'

Work blocked the images in her mind if not the pain. The day remained sober but there were moments when she was reminded that they did comfort those who needed them.

Peeta, at five, had been diagnosed with leukemia. The chemotherapy did help and his prognosis was improving. One of the first people Jacinta had seen, Peeta had been almost dead on her first day. Five days later he was eating and had even managed a laugh at Jacinta's appalling pidgin attempt to tell him a joke.

When she went back inside he was standing beside his bed, waiting for her, and she hurried over. She tilted her head questioningly, smiled and pointed to the dent on his pillow to ask why he was up.

'Me canna.'

Jacinta smiled and bent down to hug the little boy. 'That's right. You can. You are growing so strong. You so clebber.' As she knelt, with his dark head under her chin, she realized what Jonah meant. They were helping and they were needed.

For the rest of the day she seemed more aware of what Jonah did in his spare moments. Those he could help with surgery he operated on swiftly and decisively, and those who were beyond the surgeon's knife he spent more time with, sitting on their beds for a minute or two every time he passed.

And he passed often because he was everywhere. She didn't know how he did it. How he covered as much ground as he did. Supervised as much as he managed. Provided definitive care always when needed. She came to the only possible conclusion that there had to be two of him.

The morning clinic they'd missed was moved to the afternoon and they saw sixty patients before a late afternoon tea.

All three doctors barely stopped and the nurses – all Papuans – worked tirelessly towards the smooth running of the hospital. Jacinta couldn't help comparing it to Pickford's where late tea breaks constituted a disaster.

She felt marooned outside her body all of that day, watching what went on and helping where she could, yet always aware of Jonah as he worked tirelessly, and a part of her knew that he was aware of her. It was almost as if he sensed her need to be linked to someone who knew where she came from and how she thought.

By the end of the day she was mentally as well as physically exhausted and slipped away to her room to lie on her bed. She stared at the six-inch lizard that crawled up the wall in her bedroom and wished she'd never come here.

She wanted her father and Noni, her safe house and to never think of this place again. But even if she'd had the first two she knew the third would never happen.

She suspected Jonah recognized her dilemma.

He'd told her it was common for the volunteers to have sudden bouts of homesickness, especially after such a graphic example of how different this world was from the one they were used to.

When he knocked on her screen door she was slow to open it, hoping the puffiness around her eyes from her tears had gone. Maybe he'd think she'd been asleep, but when he saw her face she knew he knew.

'May I come in?'

Her eyes flickered with surprise; he was so darn particular about segregation between the staff, and then she stood back to allow him to enter. She remained standing in the centre of the room and kept her gaze on her hands.

'Let me guess.' He smiled and stepped up to her, and with a gentle finger he tilted her chin so he could see her eyes. 'You'd like a magic carpet that would pop you safely in your bed in Sydney away from all the horrible things you've seen here.'

'Yes.' Her voice sounded ridiculously small.

His eyes were shadowed. As if unable to help himself, he bent his head and brushed her lips with his own. That same sweetness was there and she resisted the urge to throw herself at him and seek the comfort she needed. The urge was strong.

'I know,' he said. 'It's hard not to dwell on this morning. Acknowledge the feelings and then let them go. That way they'll pass and then you'll go on, stronger and more determined to not be cast down by outside influences.'

'But what if I'm not strong enough?' Her biggest fear surfaced.

He actually smiled. 'You?' He pulled her face into his chest and hugged her. 'I can see your strength. You're one of the strongest women I know. You just haven't tested yourself lately. Be gentle and it will come.'

He put her away from him and stepped back because suddenly the air crackled between them. Last night had nothing on this emotion-charged need to reassure themselves that despite the girl's death they were both very much alive.

As if he read her thoughts he said quietly, 'Pudjip is not the place for liaisons.'

She knew it.

What simmered between them was no light fling. He wasn't a man a woman like her could walk away from. An affair with Jonah would be like a tropical cyclone and the strength of it would change the countryside of her life forever.

He said, 'I'll see you in the morning. After clinic, I thought we might take a drive to the local market. You haven't seen much of the village and it's only a week until we leave for the Sepik. You could brush up on your pidgin.'

Jacinta watched him let himself out with mixed feelings.

She followed him to the door and locked it after him because she knew he would listen to check that she did. She frowned at herself. No. She locked it because it was sensible to stay safe.

He'd offered her a treat like a homesick child. A lollipop of local pageantry. That was how he thought of her. In need of diversion.

What had he said? Living the high life. Which was a joke between her long hours at Pickford Emergency department and the youth refuge where she offered women's health clinic and contraception advice.

For a moment she'd hoped he was going to crush her to him, and she'd felt her body lean towards his. The irony was that she'd wanted it more than him.

It wasn't to be.

He was right. This was not a place for liaisons. She was just one of the volunteers who came and went for a week or a month or a few months, and life would go on after she went home. He'd pushed her away. Gently, it was true, but without any room for misunderstandings. She was tired but maybe it was time to think.

What the heck was she doing here?

The next morning the sun rose on another glorious day and Jacinta smiled her way through the ward rounds with Jonah and then the outpatient clinic. She really did need to remember that she was here for the medical experience. Jonah was just a mostly friendly face in her environment and a great doctor from whom she could learn.

Driving to the market with him later, it was harder to remember that.

The sun shone through the window of the Jeep onto his hands as he capably maneuvered the vehicle around the bends, and despite her attempts to divert her mind she remembered the strength and comfort those same hands had offered when he'd held her.

He turned his head and said something she didn't catch then laughed. His eyes crinkled at the comers and his beautiful mouth softened with delight, and the sight pierced her heart with regret.

'I'm sorry. I missed that,' she said, but really she wanted him to smile like that again and warm the chilled areas she couldn't seem to warm in her soul. He didn't oblige but how could he know her need? She didn't understand it herself.

'What's wrong, Jacinta? You've been very quiet this morning. Is the tragedy of yesterday still playing on your mind?'

'I think so.' It was easier to say yes than to say: Your kiss is on my mind. Your body is on my mind. I think I'm falling in love with you. She blinked and hurriedly turned her head to look sightlessly out of the window. Her mouth dried and a flare of panic fluttered in her stomach. It wasn't true. Couldn't be true.

The thought had dashed into her mind and she tried desperately to scrub the concept of considering such a thing, but the echoes of the panic wouldn't go away. The scenery dashed past the window and even the produce-laden locals walking the beaten road towards the market passed unseen by her.

Impossible relationship.

That was all they could ever have. There was no future for them, with Jonah living only for Pudjip while she had her own family and her own full life in Sydney. She could never leave all that she had achieved and place herself under the control of any man. Even Jonah.

'So, tell me about the markets. Are they big? How much further is it?' She began to babble, burying the thoughts under words that tripped over themselves, but he didn't seem to notice.

'If you're thinking Paddy's Markets in Sydney, it's nothing like that. Where we're going, the women gather in the center of the village and trade their handicrafts and food while the men gossip. You have to haggle for a bargain or they'll be disappointed.' He looked across at her. 'Do you have any money on you?'

She nodded, still in shock from her thoughts, but more confident she could control her wayward feelings. 'Carla's cousin exchanged some for me.' The quicker they arrived at some distraction, the better.

The village lay tiny and baking in dry dust in the center, but the huts were circular buildings, well made, and the view across the mountains proved spectacular. Vibrant green foliage came within a few feet of the edge of the village. The dirt road ran through the center and dozens of colorful locals were raucously gathered as they gesticulated with thin, enthusiastic arms as they bartered.

The bright feathers and headscarves of the men and women stood out in the dark-skinned crowd and the sun beat down on Jacinta's hair as she climbed out of the car. The sight differed so much from what she'd left behind. Full of excitement and free from tragedy, and she felt the burden of her thoughts lighten as the overwhelming distractions drew her attention this way and that. A good choice to come.

Children swerved in and out of the crowd, laughing and skipping with excitement, and when they saw Jonah they crowded around, grinning at him and pulling on his hands.

He laughed and as she watched he picked up a little girl of about five and hugged her and then swung her around to face Jacinta. 'This is Genna. Say hello to Missy-Dokkta.'

Genna tucked her face into Jonah's shoulder and giggled with shy delight.

'Genna had a ruptured appendix and we had to fight to save her.' He hugged her again. 'But she's fighter.' He put the little girl down, pulled some sweets from his pocket and proceeded to call each of the children by name. He pointed to Jacinta.

'Missy-Dokkta come look see.'

'Hello, Dokkta,' they choroused and crowded around her, and suddenly she was being pulled towards the market area in a group of laughing children. She looked back over her shoulder at Jonah and he was smiling with an expression in his eyes she hadn't seen before.

When the children left her, she wandered up and down the row of vendors and admired the handicrafts the women had created. She bought three empty but beautiful string bags in greens and gold that the native women filled with produce and strapped to their foreheads to keep their hands free. One was for Noni, one for her stepsister Nanette and one for herself. As she gathered more trinkets and gifts, Jacinta slid the strap around her head and carried her purchases that way too.

As a means of carrying things, the bag hung with remarkable comfort down her back from her forehead. She bought two small Hagen masks, one in a dark wood with shells for eyes for her father, and one hand-painted in ochres which she thought Noni's son Harley might like.

Tucked away on a carpet, a lovely carved pot, intricately painted in golds and brown and made out of a coconut, drew Jacinta's attention. The tiny fitted lid with button-shaped handle leant extra elegance to the shape. She admired the object several times but she couldn't decide whether to buy it.

'Do you fancy that?' Jonah appeared behind her and he draped an arm over her shoulder. 'You'll start rumors with that one.'

She smiled up at him and guiltily savored the teasing note in his voice and the weight of his arm on her shoulder. 'What is it?'

'It's a fertility gourd. The witchdoctor fills it with magic herbs for a price to make a fertility potion.'

She laughed at him. 'Do you believe in that?'

'Of course not.' He picked it up and admired it. 'It's very pretty, though.' He turned to the toothless old woman who'd made it and matched the wicked grin on her face with one of his own. 'She'll take it,' he said in pidgin.

He handed it to Jacinta with a flourish and laughed at her confusion. Then he left her to talk to a tall native man with a wooden leg, and she could hear his laugh ring out with something the man said to him.

They left not long after that and Jacinta watched the spectacular greens of the foliage close on the village and then begin to blur past her window back to the compound. It had been good to get away for the morning and she knew she would savor these memories shared with Jonah.

'Did you enjoy that?' Jonah asked indulgently.

'Very much.' She smiled at him. 'You're very popular with the children.'

'Children have good taste.'

'Spare me. Conceited man. I saw you bribe them.' He laughed and she became quiet as they drove. Oh yes. Jonah Armstrong would be a hard man to forget.

The next morning Jonah was his normal bossy self. Just after rounds began, a call came through for help in the delivery room where an older mother was in the final stages of labor. When they arrived, the mother's water had broken and the tiny buttocks of her baby were sitting curled on his mother's perineum as if testing the waters outside his haven.

Jacinta's eyes widened and Jonah whistled before moving over to the scrub sink. 'The best thing with a breech is to leave well alone,' he said over his shoulder. 'Pop your gloves on and I'll guide you.

'Most of the time a breech baby will sort itself out. You should do this delivery in case you're on your own next time.'

Jacinta hesitated. 'I've only done my obstetric rotation in my training. I didn't specialize in obstetrics.'

He grinned. 'Neither did I, but our obstetrician isn't here today.'

Jacinta nodded and swallowed the feeling of trepidation in her throat, but Jonah's words appeared prophetic. The baby's body gradually appeared with the help of gravity and his mother's efforts. Soon the baby's hips descended and it became apparent there was a new male in the family as a tiny scrotum swung into view.

As they prepared for the birth, first one and then the other of the baby's legs dropped down so that the waist and a stretched part of the umbilical cord appeared.

'People used to ease that loop of cord out to save strain on it, but now we're taught to leave it in case we cause spasm in the cord.'

Jonah spoke softly at her shoulder and she watched a section of the slippery rope slip out of the birth canal. All Jacinta needed to do was rest her hand under the baby's belly and wait.

'Makes sense,' she said. In fact, it all made sense and her exhilaration mounted.

Jonah went on softly, 'Make sure you keep the spine upwards. If the presenting part looks like rotating to belly up, you need to keep gentle traction on the baby's pelvis by holding the upper legs with your curled fingers and resting your thumbs on the dimples of the pelvis.

That prevents you from squeezing any abdominal organs if you got excited and tried to pull.'

'I promise I won't try to pull.' Jacinta slipped her fingers into position as Jonah had instructed, and he laughed softly.

'Never doubted it,' he said. 'That's where people get into trouble, though, by pulling before the umbilicus descends, because it makes the baby extend his head or pop an arm up. That's the last thing you want.'

The baby's trunk delivered quickly and Jacinta allowed the infant to rotate slightly to the left as the natural curves of the mother's pelvis facilitated delivery of first one shoulder and arm and then rotated the other way so that the other arm came free.

Finally, only the baby's head remained to be born.

She glanced across at Jonah, who nodded and demonstrated in the air how she should support the baby and allow the baby to rest on her forearm until the nape of the neck appeared.

'Breech babies really don't have a long time to mold their heads through the pelvis and I like to slow delivery of the head for that reason. Put your fingers like this.'

Jonah encouraged one of her hands under the baby's face to place one of her fingertips on each side of the little boy's cheekbones and with her other hand have fingers spread over shoulders and nape of his neck to prevent his head from being born too quickly.

'What's next?' Jonah prompted.

'Now we can lift his legs up slowly and the face will be born by the baby slowly lifting his chin as his head goes through the pelvis.' The baby did as they expected and suddenly it was over.

'My first breech delivery,' she whispered, as she laid the baby on his mother's stomach.

Jonah looked on but then his eyes widened and a slow smile spread across his face. 'Don't go away because the second one is about to come.'

The second twin was also a frank breech and again two little buttocks presented and another little scrotum. Jacinta couldn't help a tiny laugh as again the procedure was accomplished easily. 'So why do we do so many Caesareans for breech presentation in Australia?'

'Because here the mothers come to hospital a lot later in labor than they do in Pickford.'

Jacinta delivered the second placenta and Jonah was quick to massage the mother's stomach. The idea was to encourage the placental site on her uterus to clamp down to prevent hemorrhage.

He asked a question of the mother and she answered in heavy pidgin that Jacinta couldn't follow. 'Kea has only been here for fifteen minutes because she walked from twenty miles away.'

Jacinta's mouth dropped open and she laughed. 'That's one way to keep off the bed in labor.'

Both babies were close to five pounds and the mother didn't seem perturbed that there were two. 'Kea has had twins before so she'll probably go home tomorrow. I doubt the babies will have problems. This is her ninth pregnancy, so I'm more worried that she'll bleed.'

He spoke to both the nurse and Kea and nodded encouragingly as both babies were put to the breast. 'Hopefully an early breastfeed by these guys will release more oxytocin and keep her uterus well contracted.'

When Jacinta had washed, Jonah gave last instructions to the nurse and they returned to the other side of the hospital. They didn't make it to the wards.

Intercepted by the emergency department nurse, Jonah took off at a trot and Jacinta, who hadn't understood the message, followed him.

When they arrived, the ward was filled with people, many circling aimlessly with bloodied hands and heads and broken limbs.

A utility truck had overturned going up a mountain, and the men riding in the back had been tipped onto the road. Luckily nobody had been killed, but the noise was horrendous as the victims tried to make themselves heard.

With a short, sharp command Jonah silenced the majority of the voices and gestured to Jacinta to move to his side.

'Triage them, will you? I'll start here because this fellow needs a chest drain for a pneumothorax, but the others seem stable. Make sure Nurse hasn't missed anything major.'

The next two hours saw a procession of patients pass through as Jacinta splinted and padded wounds until she could get around to suturing those that needed it. Only one young man required an anesthetic while the others were stitched and plastered in the emergency ward and then discharged.

Jacinta and Jonah looked at each other as the last man departed, and both smiled. 'Now, that was a little more like a Monday morning in Pickford,' she said as she stripped off her gloves.

'You're even getting better with your pidgin. I think you'll enjoy the change when we go on our field surgery.'

Jonah

Jonah wondered if he was going to enjoy it. Usually he relished the trek, but this time he knew he'd be conscious of Jacinta every step of the way. At least here in the hospital he could keep her safe in the compound and get away if he found himself spending too much time watching her.

If he accepted she was inside his heart, he would never survive if anything happened to her. He'd made a pact many years ago to never get serious about a woman and he couldn't afford to change that now. But this trip had people waiting for them, he had to go, and he thought she'd be safer than leaving her here without him.

On the trek they'd be together from necessity, and he'd be watching her for other reasons. He wondered if it was too late to change plans.

'What are you thinking?'

Her voice broke into his thoughts and he didn't meet her eyes. 'About the trip next week.'

'You looked very grim,' she said.

He rubbed the back of his neck. He'd known she was tenacious. 'I'm wondering if perhaps it would be better if you stayed here.'

Jacinta lifted her head. 'I thought we agreed I was going with you.' The light of battle in her eyes was clear and he marveled at the difference from the shattered woman of two nights ago.

'It won't be fun. And as well as possible threat from the locals, however rare, it's an insect and wild animal fest that makes this place look like a five-star hotel.'

She glared at him and he had to suppress a smile at her ferocity. 'If I'd wanted a five-star hotel I would have stayed in Sydney. Tell me about the Sepik.'

'The Sepik?' The memories filled his mind and he could almost smell the heavy river odors and feel the dampness of the river air on his skin. 'There's nowhere like it. As you know, it's to the north of us and covers an extensive area. The river winds through the jungle and the huge tracts of marshes and crocodile-infested lowlands provide a home for aggressive wild pigs and snakes.'

Her eyebrows lifted and she murmured, 'Snakes? I may be from Australia, but I still prefer not to meet them.'

He grinned, glad to find something she couldn't romanticize. 'Definitely snakes.' He went on. 'The villages hug the river's edge and the houses are built on stilts to accommodate the rise and fall of the river. The thing I remember most is the number of canoes. All sizes, from one for the smallest child to larger family craft, all tied below each house to stakes. And it's stinking hot and the mosquitoes are vicious. I think that's where I picked up my dose of malaria last time.'

'I'm covered and I'll be careful. What about the clinics?'

'The clinics are crowded. People travel for days to see the doctors and the equipment we have is never extensive enough to cover all the needs. But some we can help and it's those successes that drag me back every time.'

'You need me with you.' She said it quietly and they both knew it was true.

He weakened, as he'd feared he would. 'I know.' But he sighed. 'I'll have to leave the arrangements as they are. I'm going back to check on Kea, you go on to lunch and I'll see you soon.'

She nodded and he watched her walk away.

She was occupying more of his thoughts each day, especially since he'd kissed her, and he needed more control. The trouble was, every time he deliberately set up distance between them something happened and he found himself wanting to hold her in his arms. Odd how the other doctors didn't end up there, he thought cynically.

Jonah shook his head and turned left towards the delivery rooms. Just over two weeks until she was gone.

Surely he could maintain the barriers for two more weeks.

Jacinta

The morning they left Pudjip the sun shone innocently through the foliage above and the breeze was light as they drove the winding Highland Highway to Mt Hagen at a clipping pace.

The Missionary Air Fellowship plane would fly the team to Wewak and then onto Hauna village, where they would take dugout canoes filled with equipment up the jungle-bordered Sepik River.

Jonah and Jacinta were accompanied by Carla and her husband Samuel, the anesthetic nurse, and they were to meet another missionary couple, Bob and Marsha Giles. Bob's specialty lay with ENT – ears, nose and throat – and Marsha a now-retired pediatrician. They made the trip every year from New York to go out with Jonah.

Like Jonah, they knew the dangers but also the rewards.

An hour outside Hagen, in one of the more desolate spots, they found the road blocked by a fallen tree. Samuel sucked in a breath, and if she wasn't mistaken Jonah had just sworn under his breath. Jacinta turned from one to the other, confused by the mixed signals and tension that had suddenly filled the vehicle.

Jonah slowed the vehicle and when they stopped both he and Samuel appeared reluctant to leave the four-wheel drive and tackle the obstacle.

'No heroics, Samuel,' Jonah ordered out of the side of his mouth, and she thought that a strange comment until four tribesmen appeared out of the jungle. Jonah put the car in reverse, but before they could turn the vehicle another four men appeared to surround it.

The leader gestured to Jonah, who opened his door and climbed out. Samuel did the same.

'Stay in the car,' he said to the women, and Carla nodded as she watched the renegades circle both men.

The leader and Jonah struck up a spirited discussion and judging by the vigorous negative from Jonah he didn't agree with the new plans. When the natives raised their axes towards the women in the car, Jonah fell silent and put his hand out to stop Samuel from flinging himself on the raiders.

The icy trickle of dread settled in Jacinta's stomach when she heard Jonah make his decision. 'I'll go with them. Get in the car, Samuel.'

Samuel shook his head and one of the men stepped forward and hit the side of Samuel's head with the flat of his axe as an incentive to comply. Samuel slid bonelessly to the ground and before Jonah could move there was a sharpened spear under his throat to prevent him interfering.

Helplessly he watched as Carla screamed and sprang from the car to her husband's side. Jacinta slid across the seat to help Carla, and the two women dragged the semi-conscious man into the back seat of the Land Rover.

Jonah called across the noise to Jacinta, 'Drive back to Pudjip. Chuck will know who to contact.'

The headman gestured at Jacinta, and Jonah vehemently shook his head, but the other man wouldn't give in. Two of the younger tribesmen approached the car with their spears and gestured for her to get out.

Jonah's face looked carved from stone. His eyes were narrowed and his mouth compressed into a thin straight line as he weighed their options. In the end even she knew there was nothing they could do to prevent her being taken, and a greater risk in resistance.

'They say if you don't come they will kill Carla and Samuel. One of them knows you're a doctor, and they say they will let us go as soon as we have done what they ask. Bring what medical gear we can carry and send Carla and Samuel back to the hospital.'

Jacinta glanced at the two men pointing spears at her, the one who held the spear to Jonah's throat and Carla's frightened face. She balled her fists to stop her hands from shaking and struggled to clear her mind as she gathered two small medical kits from the large amount they'd planned to take to the Sepik. As an afterthought she tossed in their personal antimalarials and water-purifying tablets.

The men with spears gestured for her to hurry, and she zipped up the bags and made her way over to Jonah. As soon as the two prisoners were together the party moved off in single file into the jungle. Jacinta couldn't believe her world had changed so quickly.

Jonah, close behind her, spoke quietly, and his voice was reassuring. 'It should be okay. One of their people is sick but he's wanted by the authorities and they don't want to risk him being caught at the hospital.'

'Won't kidnapping us cause more of a police presence?'

'I wish,' he said dryly. 'Not for a while. Things move slowly up here. Unless they kill us.' He went on, 'It hasn't happened in the past six years, but the usual scenario is that our mission will negotiate for our release. The best solution is that we save the patient, they send us back, the mission will have an apology from the tribe and we'll all pretend to be good friends again.'

She couldn't believe he was so calm. 'Has this happened to you before?'

'Twice.'

'No wonder you didn't want me to come.'

'Der.' His childish response made Jacinta's lips twitch, and she decided that if Jonah could make light of their situation then so could she. Or at least she could pretend to.

The men weren't angry or needlessly cruel towards her, but their tolerance was another story. If she slowed for any reason then the point of a spear would leave her in no doubt that she needed to move faster.

After half an hour she'd begun to find it more difficult to keep up the pace. She heard Jonah speak to one of their captors and her pack was taken and handed to Jonah. Despite her reluctance to doubly burden him, she sighed with relief.

'Thank you,' she muttered over her shoulder, and her mouth felt dry and coated and her voice croaked a little.

He must have heard the struggle she was having. 'We'll stop soon because there's a ravine we have to cross. Don't look down when we cross the rope bridge and watch out for vines or you'll trip. There's a waterfall not much further after that.'

'Do you know the place we're going to?'

'I've a fair idea for the first hour, but after that it will be new territory.'

'How long do you think it will be?'

'No idea. When we get there they'll let you rest. Keep your head down and don't aggravate them. Though if you get a good chance to escape, take it, and don't worry about me. It will be easier to escape one at a time than together. Don't even think about me because I'll be fine.'

Jacinta listened to his words but she never thought she'd act on them. The thought of being out here on her own gave her no comfort.

When they arrived at the camp it was easy to see the tribe weren't planning on staying long.

There were about a dozen ragged tents and lean-tos made out of tarpaulins pegged to the ground around center poles, a few straggling chickens, two fire pits and a huddle of women peeling some kind of root vegetable on the outskirts.

Jonah, carrying the medical supplies, was taken to the chief and Jacinta found herself pushed inside an empty tent. She could see the legs of the guard outside the entrance and stifled a half-hysterical laugh. She doubted she needed watching as she wasn't planning on walking off anywhere.

With her back against the central support, Jacinta slid down the shaft of the roughly hewn wood and settled her bottom on the ground to rest her shaking legs. She shut her eyes.

Images of Jonah being beaten or killed crowded her mind, but she kept telling herself that Jonah had been in this kind of situation before. She didn't dare think about being left alone with the tribesmen if anything happened to Jonah.

Her thoughts made for a fitful rest but she must have dozed off because the light seemed different when she woke at Jonah's entrance. She tried to scramble up and almost fell over again from her previously cramped position. Thank God he was safe.

Jonah

For Jonah, all through the last few hours while he'd bathed the sick man's wounds and administered the few drugs he had, his mind had been on Jacinta.

His face stretched with relief when he saw Jacinta and he crouched down beside her to help her stand. Her relieved smile made his stomach jolt with relief that she was fine. She looked tired but in none of the distress he'd feared as he'd waited to be brought to her.

His repeated questions to the chief had been met with bland assurances that she was safe in her tent as a guarantee that Jonah would save the chief's son.

As the night had worn on and little improvement had been seen in the patient, the chief had begun to mutter dire warnings about what would happen to the Missy-Dokkta if Jonah failed.

Thankfully, at last, in the early hours of the morning, the patient had seemed to rest more easily, and grudgingly the chief had allowed Jonah to be led to the creek to wash before returning to Jacinta.

Now, to find her drowsily awake after what he'd dreaded he would find, he was almost faint with relief.

His brain, already sluggish with physical and nervous exhaustion, totally scrambled and he struggled for something to divert how much he wanted to feel his arms around her.

Jacinta had no such qualms as she hurled herself at him and buried her nose in his chest. 'Thank God you're safe,' she said. Her arms crept around him and he felt himself sigh into her as he hugged her back.

Jonah buried his face in the hair on top of her head and inhaled the freshness of her after the rankness of disease and approaching death of the last six hours. His breath released another notch. 'They haven't hurt you?'

'No, I'm fine. You?'

'Just tired.'

'How's the patient?' she asked.

His smile faded. 'Dying. It would be useful if they didn't blame us when the inevitable happens.' The words hung in the tent between them, and he saw her swallow. He hadn't made that sound promising. But it wasn't. They needed to get out of here before it all went down.

Jonah put her from him and tried not to clench his hands in frustration. He knew she'd see and realize this was even more dire than she'd supposed.

'Is there nothing we can do for him?'

Of course she needed clarification though she'd be sorry she asked. But she needed to do it quietly. He rested his finger across her lips as the guard poked his head into the tent and glared at them both suspiciously. Jonah stepped in front of her but there was little comfort in the action because, no matter how skilled, one man against a dozen couldn't win.

The guard glared at him and then flopped the tent flap back into place. He could see the outline of his body as he planted his feet outside the gap. Jonah cast an assessing gaze around the makeshift tent and then back to Jacinta's worried face.

Unable to stop himself he tipped her chin up to look at him and shook his head. Spoke very quietly. 'There will be no defeat in this tent. We're in strife, no doubt about that, but opportunities always rise when you least expect them.' He went on to explain, 'Our patient, Tuma, is the chief's son. His stomach wound is gangrenous, and he needs more antibiotics than we have. I told the chief his son would die if he's not taken to the hospital.' He met her eyes. 'He told me if his son dies, we would die, too.'

She shook her head at the mention of death. Rolled her eyes in disgust. 'That's a lot of death.'

He wanted to hug her against him and not let her go. Instead he watched her beautiful eyes narrow.

'What can we do?' she asked.

He shook his head. 'No brilliant plans yet. We continue to bathe the wound, use our antibiotics, keep the patient hydrated and hope his own immune system will eventually beat the organism. But I think that will only buy us some time – if we're lucky, a couple of days – before the inevitable happens. Septicemia will kill him.'

He could hear the certainty in his own voice, but it was better his tone removed any hope Jacinta had that they would be able to treat their way out of captivity. She needed to be looking for opportunities for escape.

'You don't appear too perturbed about the chief's threat to kill us.' Her voice sounded so calm and normal, as if they were discussing putting sugar in tea. He wondered if she did understand.

'Oh, I'm perturbed,' he said dryly. 'The threat is real enough, but I'm not planning on us staying around long enough to let it happen. It's a good sign they haven't tied you up. When the moon sets in about an hour, we'll have a brief window of opportunity to get away.'

He saw her shoulders sag with relief. 'So what's the plan?'

Jonah felt the weight of her expectations on his shoulders. She stood there, unintentionally leaning towards him, his tough Jacinta suddenly fragile as she watched him, so sure he knew all the answers. His greatest fear, the thing he prayed he'd never have to face, stared him in the eye.

Here was Melinda all over again.

He felt like screaming that he didn't want this responsibility. What if he couldn't save this woman either? The thought was like a hammer raining blows between his shoulder blades and he winced at the pain.

'We'll have to wait for the opportunity when it presents itself,' he said gruffly. 'They'll wake us if Tuma takes a turn for the worse.' He paused and finished under his breath, 'Or when he dies. Maybe you should try to sleep. When we run it will be hard going in the dark.'

She tried to smile at him but her mouth wobbled at the edges. 'Thank you for saying when and not if.'

The least he could do. 'My pleasure.'

She hesitated before she lay down. 'Will you hold me?'

Reality crashed in and he closed his eyes with the pain of loss. He couldn't let this happen to her. But she was waiting for his answer. He opened his eyes, furious with himself that she'd had to ask when her need was so great.

'Yes please,' he teased softly and drew her towards him. Then he stopped. 'Wait. I'll spread this blanket. It's not the softest in the world but it beats the heck out of the dirt.'

Then he lay down beside her and she snuggled into his chest with his arm behind her head and her soft cheek on his skin. That contact seared into his heart.

Her hair smelt of some citrusy shampoo and unobtrusively he breathed in her scent more deeply. The top of her head was so close to his mouth he couldn't help the gentle kiss that he lost in the softness. That action added taste to his sensations and Jonah closed his eyes as the essence of her swirled through his body like a drug.

All the feelings he'd been suppressing since the first day he'd met her rose like a heated mist inside him. He jerked open his eyes.

It would be crazy to venture down that path, and he tipped his head back to stare at the point where the center pole met the apex of the tarpaulin. A few stars shone through the gap in the tent and between the treetops and he couldn't believe he'd contemplated making love to her. They were in mortal danger, for Pete's sake.

Diffused light from the moon shone through the rough lashing. If it rained, the hole was big enough for them to get wet. Good. He was in need of a cold shower.

Jacinta must have noticed he'd withdrawn from her because she twisted her neck to look up at him. Her invitation or need, he wasn't sure which, made a mockery of his denial and helplessly he stared back at her, weak with his own wanting.

'Kiss me.' He wasn't sure if she said it out loud or even formed the words with her lips, but the request was there and he had no defense against that appeal. When he lowered his head, her mouth under his was so sweet and their joining so achingly tender and beautiful that he knew he would never forget it. He could do nothing else but kiss her again.

A long time later they surfaced, breathless and red-cheeked as they opened their eyes.

Jonah felt as though his heart was breaking. 'I've wanted to kiss you like that for a long time. From the first moment I saw your beautiful face.'

Jacinta

She smiled, brushed a smudge of dirt from his face and doubted either of them would win any beauty pageants at the moment. But the emotion beneath his words was a thing of immense beauty, a caress whispered against her skin, and she smiled as she closed her eyes so she could forget where she was and just be, in this moment, in his arms.

She'd accepted the strange ache she'd had since Jonah Armstrong had been wheeled into her world and the futility of fighting against her destiny to love him.

Aware now why she'd followed him to this country, risking everything, and if in the end she'd gambled more than she'd planned to, it was because of this moment, and any moments they had left.

Was he her soul mate?

Was he the empty part of her heart that she'd thought would never be filled?

Here in this grubby, earthen-floored tent on a steamy, menacing night in the highlands of Papua New Guinea, she knew she'd found love. Not the floating, romantic, giggly type of love but the

I-need-him-to-breathe type of love that promised heartache and agony if they were given enough time.

Off balance and confused by the magnitude of her discovery, Jacinta hugged the questions to herself for a little longer, but she couldn't help squeezing his hand and praying that at least some of her feelings were returned.

She regretted the pain she would cause to Noni and her father at her choice to come to this country, but she could not regret her discovery.

She lifted her face to Jonah's and this time she took the initiative. The restraint of his lips softened as she pressed more firmly against him. He waited, almost passive under her mouth as if testing her resolve, until the first tentative touch from her tongue kindled his passion.

Then he shifted his weight and took control, and she was seared by his need as he crushed her to him. This time it was different, this time she found a need in him that she hadn't realized she had the power to ignite.

There was awe in that realization that made her want to push him further, but he loosened his hold and gentled his mouth before he put her away from him.

'I wish, my love, but this is not the place. Try to sleep,' he said softly. 'I want you. Don't ever doubt that. I've wanted you from the first moment 1 saw you. I just hope that when we are safely back at Pudjip you don't regret me telling you this.'

He eased over to lean above her, planted his hands on either side of her head and seared her with a look. 'You are the most amazing woman I have ever met.' He kissed her and then edged back reluctantly to sit upright against the pole. 'Sleep. I'll keep watch in case there's a chance to get away.'

Jacinta sighed with frustration as she lay back and pulled her fore-arm over her face. She'd just received her first refusal, but the way he'd refused had made her smile through her embarrassment. She didn't regret asking, only his answer. But she'd never sleep. She sat up against the pole beside him. 'I've slept. Tell me about your sister.'

'Women,' he said mockingly, but she could tell he wasn't really annoyed. 'Melinda was like an angel, naive and full of goodness and smiles. She believed in the good in everybody, and in the end it killed her. I should never have let her come here to be with me. Once she went outside the compound at night to aid someone when I was busy, and that was enough. I never saw her alive again.' His shoulders drooped and Jacinta realized he was tired. Of course he was.

'Rest, Jonah. Put your head in my lap. If only for half an hour. I'll wake you if I need you.'

The time passed slowly for Jacinta, but it was time she used to savor her new discovery – that she loved Jonah.

Soon the moon set and she woke him. When they were ready, he stood at the entrance to the tent and peered around the flap at the sleeping guard.

Jonah put his hand to his lips and motioned for her to follow, but before they could take two steps the headman that had abducted them blocked their way with his spear. He kicked the sleeping guard awake.

Almost as if he'd been expecting their escape attempt, their taller and more vigilant captor gestured for them to return to the tent.

'He was waiting.' Her voice died away as the guard entered the tent and gestured for them both to back up against the pole and sit with their hands behind their backs.

Jonah tried to reason with him but the rapid dialect was hard for Jacinta to follow and she could see the man wouldn't be swayed. He stared back implacably and gestured with his spear at Jacinta until Jonah obeyed.

Their wrists were tied and then looped together either side of the wooden pole until their shoulders touched around the pole. At least that human warmth was allowed them. The guard gave a last tug at his knots and then, satisfied he'd secured the prisoners, he left.

Jonah twined his fingers through Jacinta's for reassurance, but she knew he could feel the shudder of fear in her body. She heard him swear under his breath.

'We'll figure something out. Don't worry.' His words hung in the air and Jacinta grimaced.

No, don't worry. All will be well.

She didn't answer out loud and he squeezed her hand. 'Are you all right?'

'Even I know being tied up in a tent by a renegade tribe in the wilds of the Highlands is not a good scenario, Jonah.' Her voice wobbled less than it could have as she tried desperately to stay strong. 'But I won't fall to pieces, if that's what you're worried about.' Though she muttered under her breath, 'I'll do that later.'

'I think you're pretty wonderful, Dr McCloud.' He squeezed her hand again. 'Plus, you're a beautiful kisser.'

She squeezed his fingers back and suddenly things weren't quite so bad. 'And I wouldn't want to be tied to a pole with anyone else,' she said with pretended nonchalance. 'Now I'm going to be quiet so you can bend your fierce intellect to how we're going to get out of here.'

She could feel the tears thick in her throat and hoped he couldn't hear them in her voice.

Tomorrow would be a big day one way or another. She drifted into an uneasy doze, and every now and then she roused to feel Jonah twisting the rope they had been secured with, but there was no slack in the knots. The guard had probably been tying pigs to poles since he could walk.

Jacinta

The first hint of light crept into the tent at about the same time as sounds of the stirring camp woke Jacinta. Barely a minute later, the flap of the tent opened and an old woman followed their guard in and began to untie Jacinta's bonds.

Jonah jerked awake behind her as the old woman muttered under her breath and struggled with the twine knots. Jacinta stared at the newcomer, certain she'd seen her somewhere before.

Jonah spoke to the woman in an unfamiliar dialect, and Jacinta saw her shake her head and point to Jacinta and then herself.

'Mimi and Missy-Dokkta.' And she made a cutting motion with her hands. That's all, she seemed to say.

Jacinta remembered then. 'Mimi was in the plane that I came to Hagen in,' she said over her shoulder to Jonah. 'What did she say?'

'She said the chief's son's wife is having a baby and in trouble. You'd better go with her.'

Jacinta followed Mimi across to another tent on the outskirts of the camp and the cloying smell of blood and amniotic fluid hit her nostrils and warned her of what she'd see.

The young woman on the grass mound moaned softly as she pushed with the force of the contraction and a tiny baby's breech body, the size of a large man's hand, was suspended between life and death.

Heart in throat, Jacinta was thankful for Jonah's recent lessons, and as she came closer she worried just how premature this child was.

One thing at a time. She settled herself and glanced around for somewhere to wash her hands. Of course there were no facilities or even a dish of water so she wiped her hands on her shirt and apologized to the hygiene God as she neared the woman. How had she become the midwife in the jungle?

Anchored by his head, the baby's tiny body was mottled blue as he lay suspended between intra- and extra-uterine life. Jacinta glanced at Mimi and pointed to herself and the baby, seeking permission.

'Yes. Quick-quick.' The old woman nodded with some urgency.

Jacinta drew a deep breath. Muttering, 'So much for hands-off breech.'

Jacinta tried to smile at the half-conscious woman as she lay her down in reassurance and knelt down on the dirt. Then she realized why this baby looked different. The belly was facing upwards and the baby's head was already chin up and could not extend further to be born.

When she checked the crease in the little one's neck for a hidden umbilical cord, sure enough, the slowly pulsating rope was looped around the baby's neck as well.

'Rotate the baby from face up to face down,' she muttered to herself, 'and slip the cord over the head if you can.'

The tightness of the cord around his neck made it impossible for Jacinta to do much other than cut the lifeline prior to birth. The idea was unattractive without a clamp or even a piece of string to stop fetal hemorrhage.

'String? I need string or twine to tie the cord and a knife.' She mimed the tying off of the cord to Mimi and cutting motions.

Mimi asked around the gathered women and one of them produced a wicked-looking knife, which she handed to Jacinta. For the string, Mimi just shrugged that she didn't understand.

Jacinta felt like screaming until she calmed herself with a deep breath. Okay. Think laterally.

She gestured for Mimi to come over and grasp the umbilical cord a few inches from the baby's belly and squeeze very hard. If the maternal end of the cord bled it would not be catastrophic, but if blood drained from this tiny baby, things would quickly deteriorate. She'd think of a cord tie in a minute.

Quickly Jacinta cut the cord as far away from Mimi's fingers as she could manage and unwound the now free end from the baby's neck. As soon as the anchor was gone, she rotated the baby slowly to face down and the little boy slid out into Jacinta's hands and lay flaccidly like a stunned fish, with his dark eyes staring unblinkingly up at her.

At least the baby's end of the cord was long enough, she consoled herself as she tied one knot in the slippery rope and then another one.

'That's what I call a true knot in the cord,' she muttered to herself and concentrated on his resuscitation.

Jacinta pulled the blanket over him, rubbing his body quickly through the material to stimulate him to breathe as well as dry him. And blew a stream of her breath into his face to startle him.

His feeble cry was greeted by a sudden babble of voices and even the new mother opened her eyes and smiled before she lapsed back into her stupor.

Don't celebrate too early, Jacinta thought grimly, because she'd bet the infant was at least six weeks early and would be touch and go in such primitive conditions.

A sudden gush of blood heralded the next complication and she concentrated on the mother as the placenta was delivered. The baby could nestle between his mother's breasts while Jacinta worried about the flood of bright blood that had begun at the bottom of the makeshift bed.

Basics, she urged herself, and firmly massaged the woman's uterus through the recently stretched abdominal wall until the red torrent slowed and finally stopped. Jacinta quickly dabbed away the blood to check for tissue trauma before the next gush began. She couldn't see anything that would cause bleeding, so that left the muscular contraction of the uterus as the most likely candidate.

'Rub here.' She mimed how Mimi should find the top of the new mother's uterus and massage her abdomen to help start the contraction of the uterus and constriction of the source of bleeding.

Mimi nodded and calmly continued that job while Jacinta wiped her hands on the edge of the blanket and leaned up to peer under the blanket at the new baby. His tiny face screwed up under the thick coating of white vernix that almost glued his eyes shut, but despite his size he looked perfect.

When he let out another mewing cry Jacinta gestured to his mother's breast and mimed to another woman squeezing colostrum into the baby's mouth. If the newborn was to have any chance, he needed warmth and ideally at least a couple of mils of expressed colostrum dripped into his mouth every hour.

As she sat back on her hands her eyes fell on the bloodstained knife that rested beside her foot. It lay unnoticed by the distracted women as they cooed over the new baby.

Unobtrusively she glanced around and leaned towards the new mother. Her right hand fell down beside her leg until she found the knife. With her dominant hand Jacinta gently rubbed the mother's stomach again and curled the fingers of the other around the wooden handle. She nudged the implement slowly until it was cold and sticky inside her sock.

No doubt Mimi's friend would miss her knife, but hopefully she wouldn't connect its disappearance with Jacinta.

The baby was being cared for and there was nothing else she could do there. Jacinta avoided Mimi's eyes as she shifted position and couldn't wait to see Jonah with her prize. Her knees protested as she eased out of her cramped stance and arched her back to dissipate the tension from it.

As she looked around the circle of faces, she noticed a small girl watching her with wary eyes. Instinctively she smiled as if she hadn't just broken their trust and stolen from them. The girl glanced down at Jacinta's ankle and then away, and the cold hand of dread settled in her stomach. It had been worth a try, she consoled herself as she waited for the outbreak of recriminations.

Instead, she was congratulated by the women and Mimi pointed to the young mother and introduced her. 'Neena.'

'Congratulations, Neena,' Jacinta said to the new mother, and then she was ushered out.

She was escorted back towards their tent and nothing had been said about the knife.

Jacinta motioned towards the nearby creek and mimed washing her hands. Mimi gestured assent and followed Jacinta to the water's edge.

Crystal clear and icy cold, the water swirled away the drying blood from her fingers, and she sighed with pleasure as she dug her fingers into the sandy bottom to loosen any blood under her fingernails. She splashed her face but before she could get carried away with her ablutions Mimi poked her in the back and hurried her not unkindly back up the incline towards the tent.

At least she hadn't tied her up again, Jacinta thought as she was left alone in the tent once more. Jonah must have been recalled to duty on the chief's son. That was the only scenario her brain would allow her to contemplate, and she glanced around for a place to hide the knife in case they came back to search her.

With an effort she managed to make a thin shaft in the soil beside the wooden base of the central pole, and pushed the knife into it until the handle top was level with the surface. She dusted dirt over the top but not deeply, so that if their hands were tied again that night, hopefully Jonah would be able to retrieve it.

No sooner had she brushed her hands as free of dirt as she could, Mimi returned with a guard and the suspicion in her eyes was clear. She gestured for Jacinta to turn around and searched her thoroughly. The bloodstained sock caused no comment as there were other stains elsewhere on her clothing. Satisfied, though unhappily, that Jacinta didn't have the knife, Mimi left.

When Jonah was pushed inside the tent a few minutes later Jacinta didn't wait for an invitation as she launched herself at him. When his arms closed around her she sagged with relief and buried her head in his chest.

'I'm pleased to see you, too. What's this in aid of?' his voice rumbled from above her ear, and she breathed in the unmistakable male scent of him, comforted by the fact that he was solidly around her. She could feel the palpitations in her own chest, and the regular thump of Jonah's heart was infinitely reassuring. They were safe for the time being.

His finger slid under her chin and he tilted her face so he could see her expression. 'Are you okay?' Concern slashed his brow as if he suspected she wasn't.

'I'm fine now.' She pulled out of his arms reluctantly and stepped back, trying hard to maintain a smile. 'It was a big morning. I had some news and you weren't here.' She chewed her lip ruefully. 'And when you didn't come back, I started to worry. And then they searched me for the knife and it was pretty scary.'

'What knife?' he asked.

Typical male, Jacinta thought. Go straight to what interests you. But she was proud of her ingenuity.

'The knife I stole and buried beside the pole so we can cut our ropes tonight.'

A slow smile spread across his face and he tugged her back into his arms for a brief hug and then held her away from him to look into her face. She couldn't tell what he was thinking but there was warmth in his blue eyes.

'You continue to surprise me.' His voice dropped as he lowered his head, and then his lips touched hers and he closed his eyes as he savored the taste of her. The kiss was gentle, but conveyed a multitude of messages that confirmed he cared before he let her go. 'So many pleasant surprises,' he mused. 'Where did you get the knife?'

She told him of the birth and his enthusiastic approval did nothing to settle the tumult his kiss had stirred.

'How is Tuma?' she asked for distraction, and watched his eyes darken with concern.

'Tuma has rallied a little but I suspect his improvement is that false hope you sometimes see before a patient fades forever.'

Jacinta nodded. She'd seen it many times too. Critical patients seemed to wake and respond for a brief time before lapsing back into unconsciousness, never to wake again.

'How much time do you think we have?'

Jonah met her look squarely, and she was glad because she deserved the truth even though she knew he was reluctant to worry her. 'Tonight – tomorrow at the latest. But it's a catch twenty-two situation. If we escape, our trail has to be a couple of hours old for them not to risk following us, so we need to pick our moment to run.'

SEVERAL hours after dark, when the night birds began their raucous cries for food, there was a commotion in the camp. A sudden lone female wailed loudly in grief and then the mournful sound swelled as more voices acknowledged someone's passing.

Jonah met Jacinta's eyes as he moved over to the entrance to listen to the guards' conversation. He nodded as if he'd already known. 'Tuma is dead.'

Dread settled over her as his words sank in and he moved back to support her. She sagged against him. Then moistened her lips to form the words she dreaded asking. 'When... when will they come for us?'

His face looked so grim she knew the answer before he uttered the one word. 'Soon.'

There was no time to plan any kind of resistance or flight. The entrance flap to the tent was yanked back and a tribesman gestured for them both to follow him. This time the point of his spear was less reticent about hurting them and pricked their backs as they were nudged none too gently towards the chief's hut.

Jacinta felt the eeriness of recent death crossing the camp. Campfires burned in several places, and the women and children huddled together as they keened outside their tents. Stone-faced tribesmen stared implacably at the white doctors who had failed their chief and his son. There was no comfort to be had on the trek to hear their fate.

The chief's head hung bowed when they entered the tent and Jacinta could smell the infection that had killed Tuma. The young man's body lay still and silent.

The chief launched into a tirade against Jonah, the words hurled like stones in his grief, the accusations and waving of arms angrily denying any use from the white man who stared back expressionless until the old man finished.

Jacinta struggled to pick up a few of the rapidly spoken words and those she recognized struck fear into her heart.

Jonah's expression didn't change and Jacinta prayed she'd misinterpreted. If anything, the chief's grief increased as Jonah chose his words. His tone was quiet and even, as if dealing with a fractious patient. He paused and drew Jacinta next to him, until she stood firm against his side, united with Jonah against the old man.

The chief shrugged, spat and grunted, and then turned away from them. The guard that had accompanied them gestured for them to leave.

'Tell me,' Jacinta whispered as they were prodded back to their tent.

'The chief says we die when the sun rises tomorrow.'

The words were no less horrific for the quiet way they were spoken, but something didn't make sense. 'I heard him say "now".'

Jonah smiled grimly. 'He did, but I suggested we at least deserved another night alive together.'

There was something about the way he said "together" that seemed to hold a key to the chief changing his mind, and she mulled it over as they crossed the now-deserted camp.

Jonah

Jonah admired that her back remained unbowed as she walked, and he ached with how much she'd come to mean to him. She was worthy of a better man than he, but she wouldn't have that chance now.

No sign of hysterics, though probably it was her misguided blind faith that he'd still find a way out of this mess. His fists clenched with frustration. He was all out of ideas at the moment. Even now, they had been so close to immediate death that he couldn't believe they had a stay of execution.

He needed to gather his reserves for the next fight. His heart ached with regret because he knew there was little he could do now that the chief had decreed their death. The old man would be doubly suspicious that they would try to escape.

Jacinta ducked inside the tent in front of him. 'We have to escape.'

Jonah saw her glance around the tent for inspiration and he wished he could comfort her. She was so full of life and had so much to offer, both as a doctor and a woman, let alone the anguish of knowing she would never see her family again. He should have left her at the hospital where at least she had the compound to keep her safe.

If there was some way he could get her to safety, it didn't matter if he didn't make it. No one was waiting for him at home.

He'd tried. That first day he'd asked the chief to let her go and he would gladly stay, but the old man had had none of it.

Tonight he'd offered everything he could imagine to sway the chief from killing Jacinta. Money and medicinal drugs – which he'd never have believed he'd even pretend to promise. But the old man had been adamant they should pay for Tuma's death.

Jacinta clenched her hands. 'So that's it? We just sit here and wait for them to come and kill us in the morning? It seems so bizarre. So pointless. Is there nothing we can do in the meantime?'

He shrugged. 'We can fight now, I could probably hurt or kill one or two of them, but before you could run they would cut us both down, and I'd rather not have their blood on my hands for no reason. Even if they leave us untied, it will be difficult as they've put more guards outside the tent.

'Maybe the men will sleep in the early hours of the morning so that we can slip away, but it will be much harder now that Tuma is dead.'

'Why would they leave us untied when they tied us last night?'

'Does it matter?' He didn't meet her eyes. Should he tell her it was because the chief had agreed he could make her his wife before the morning?

Jonah didn't know why he'd suggested it to the old man, but the request had at least worked temporarily. It had helped when he'd reminded the chief of Jacinta's part in saving his grandson.

'Our only chance is to sneak away when the camp is asleep.' He didn't say it but at the moment he could see very little hope of that. No guard would risk a newly bereaved chief's wrath by sleeping and allowing the prisoners to escape – especially having been caught the previous night.

He needed to regather his mental energy, battle this inertia that was seeping into him. He hadn't slept at all last night, terrified that some of the men would come and take Jacinta for sport, but it hadn't happened. He needed clarity of mind to plan their escape if he could just forget the danger to Jacinta for a while.

'We have time to pass before we can even think about doing anything. They will leave us alone for the time being.'

She looked up suspiciously. 'How do you know that?'

He pretended to frown. 'Why do you have to ask questions?'

She wasn't fooled. 'There's something suspicious about a death sentence and no bonds and something not genuine about a twelve-hour reprieve. And there's something you're not telling me.'

He looked into her eyes then and a gentle smile hovered where no smile should be. 'True.'

He watched her take in his admission and she turned away before he could read what conclusion she'd drawn. That was the truth – she was far from slow-witted. 'What are you not telling me?'

She wouldn't give up, but then, he'd known she wouldn't. 'That you are tenacious and annoying and brilliant and a great doctor, and you scare the living daylights out of me.'

She may as well know the lot.

The rest he said slowly. 'The last person I loved died in this country, too, and I can't bear the thought of not being able to save you either. I told the chief that he owed it to us to give us one more night together, and he agreed.'

She blinked back the tears that his words triggered and bit her lip.

He brushed her cheek with his finger. 'Is there any chance of one of those kisses we had last night? I'm sorely in need of a little comfort and you are so very good at making me feel better.'

Jacinta

Jacinta blinked and, despite his banter, she could hear the need in his words.

He needed her!

The concept was harder to comprehend than Pidgin English. Did Jonah mean he cared for her? At the very least it was proof her feelings weren't one-sided, and through all the fear and uncertainty today, at the back of her mind the memory of last night's closeness had sustained her.

Then his previous words sank in. The last time he'd loved someone – that meant he loved someone now. Her?

He opened his arms. 'Come here and kiss me.' It was almost an order.

In another time and place she might have wanted to continue the argument, explore the beginnings of wonder that they loved each other. Maybe banter with him and pit her wits against his. But the time wasn't right. Every moment was precious now and she stepped into his embrace with a sigh of relief.

His hand brushed the hair from her forehead as he looked deep into her eyes, and she absorbed the sight of his dear face like dry earth absorbing rain.

'In another time and place I won't always come so placidly, you know,' she whispered as he came closer.

'I'll look forward to it,' he said, and his mouth brushed hers. There was no further inclination for talking as their needs rose in a swell of emotion that lifted them both away from their circumstances and transported them to a much sweeter place.

But they couldn't stay there forever. A shout from outside the tent reminded them of their danger and they stepped apart. A guard pulled back a quarter of the gap and slid a drooping leaf with fruit and a mug of water onto the floor beside the entrance.

Jacinta stared fearfully at the man but he didn't meet her eyes as he backed out. She buried her face in Jonah's chest again as her heart rate settled and she accepted that the tribesmen hadn't changed their minds about the time to kill them yet. 'We've wasted so much time and there's so little left,' she said.

'We should eat because we'll need our strength.'

'Why would they feed us when they want to kill us?'

He crouched down beside the offering and began to divide the fruit. 'They are being polite.'

Jacinta shook her head. 'Can't they be rude and not kill us?'

'Good plan.'

Jacinta sighed. 'You've changed again and I don't understand you.'

'We still have the rest of the night to get away, we have to focus on that. We have your knife, we have each other and we have several hours to wait, and then we escape before it starts getting light. But I'm so tired I can hardly see straight.'

She saw it then.

The burden he carried, the fear that was mostly for her, and the strain as he racked his brain for a solution to their predicament. She could share some of his responsibilities, if only for a short while. She moved over to crouch beside him. 'We'll eat, and we'll lie down together, and then you sleep for a little while and I'll keep watch.'

'Doctor's orders, Jacinta?' The weariness was there behind his smile and she knew he couldn't refuse.

'Absolutely. Rest, Jonah.'

Their eyes met, held, drew comfort from each other, and then met again while they ate their fruit and slaked their thirst.

When they were finished, Jonah pushed the remains outside the tent to prevent the risk of any stray animals searching the tent to forage. She gathered their things as if ready for flight. If they escaped, the medicines they had were too precious to leave.

Half an hour later, with his head in her lap, Jonah breathed deeply in sleep and the harsh lines in his face relaxed as he entrusted their safety to her.

Jacinta sat upright against the pole and listened to the sound of the camp settling around them, and every few minutes the guards outside their tent grunted to each other.

Jacinta's mind roved over the last few weeks and the strange emotions she'd felt at each new experience. She had such huge admiration for the hospital staff and the missionaries, and despite the horror of the brutality she'd seen, there was such beauty in the tropical nights and the simplicity and innocence of the children. Everything seemed so much larger than life here.

But nothing was larger in her life than Jonah.

As he slept, she memorized his face. His strong nose and jaw, his long lashes hiding those blue eyes she could lose herself in. In repose she wanted to stroke his face but she dare not interrupt his precious rest.

Instead she wondered at the boy he must have been before he'd turned into the responsible man he'd become. Was there a time he'd been carefree or had he always been bowed with the misfortunes of others and his role in their care?

What had his parents been like? What exactly had happened to his sister?

He ran the hospital not like the dictator she'd first thought, although he certainly expected to be obeyed, but like an older brother. He kept his finger on the pulse not just of his patients but all his staff and their families, too. He needed to delegate more, realize that others could carry the load he shouldered too often on his own.

Like he shouldered the responsibility of getting them out of here, but there was no reason she couldn't think up just as good an escape plan as he could.

Jacinta glanced around the dark tent again, straining for inspiration. Perhaps if she listed their assets, an idea would come to her. She had nothing else to do.

Their main asset was Jonah. He was experienced, brave, knew the area and their captors, and hopefully when he woke he would be refreshed enough to sort out any details of the great plan she would come up with.

Their second asset was the knife – something their captors didn't know they had.

Their third was the medicine kit.

Her eyes shifted to the tote she'd packed in preparation for their escape. It was a possible resource she hadn't given a lot of thought to, but she could remedy that short-sightedness now.

Jacinta stretched her arm carefully across and grasped the handle of the rucksack, anxious not to disturb Jonah's sleep as he lay with his head in her lap. He stirred with her sideways movement and his eyelids flickered with the slight dragging noise the bag made as it bumped across towards her.

Instinctively she stroked his brow and he sighed and settled back into slumber without opening his eyes.

Quietly, when the bag rested against her hip, she began to pull out the contents one by one and place them on the dirt floor beside her. She could just make out the objects in the dark. There must be something here that could help.

Their water-purifying and antimalarial tablets and the vial of salt for leeches lay on top. Then the tourniquet, cannulas and intravenous tubing to run a drip, a bag of saline, some sticking plaster, dressings and two bandages. The tiny blood-pressure cuff and stethoscope had potential as they were made up of several components, some of which surely could be useful.

She rummaged at the bottom of the bag and found a penlight she'd forgotten about and the zippered compartment of drug ampoules and tablets.

The only anesthetic drugs they had were short-acting muscle re-laxants and she mulled over the logistics of administering a drug to someone without them becoming aware of the fact. Fancifully she saw herself injecting a guard with an anesthetic through the lining of the tent. Perhaps he'd brush the sting away like a mosquito. Perhaps he'd run her through with his spear.

She really was better equipped to deal with the concrete jungle of Sydney.

She rummaged through the last of the drugs. There were antihy-pertensives, Adrenalin for shock, Valium for fits and two ampoules of

Morphine for pain. All in all a slim selection, but not without some capacity to help their cause.

Apart from the logistics of administration, if they could render the guards unconscious, they could slit the back of the tent and escape into the night. Her mind twisted and darted through scenarios of escape, and the time passed.

When Jonah woke the hut was dark, but without seeing him she knew his features as if it were midday in the sun. Unless a miracle arrived – or the cavalry – she suspected they would die in a few hours. She just hoped it would be swiftly. For both of them.

'Come down here, Jacinta.'

She looked down at his open eyes and smiled. His tone was more tender than she'd ever heard and it was too dark to read his face. She snuggled down beside him and rested her head on his arm, which he tucked beneath her.

'Our escape hasn't gone to plan and there's a chance we may not make it home,' he said. 'There are things that should be said between us should anything happen.'

Jacinta was jerked right out of her heroic daydreams. 'What happened to waiting for the fat lady to sing? What happened to never give up?'

'Of course we won't give up, and I'll protect you with my life. If an opportunity arises, we take it, but this is about us and about something that can't be changed, no matter what happens in the morning.'

His big hands lifted and cupped her face. The calloused palms warm and reassuring against her cheeks.

'I know it's very soon but I need to tell you that I love you.' In the darkness his words brushed her skin with the depth of his feeling. This was truth. As if he'd heard her thoughts, 'I've never said that romantically to another woman in my entire life. I love your strengths and your weaknesses and your beauty and your feistiness.' He hugged her to him. 'I love all of you.'

It was too tragic and heartbreaking and she couldn't quite believe him because look where they were. What could she say? How could she respond?

She focused on the one thing that rankled. 'I don't have weaknesses.'

'Only moments of surrender, my love, which I plan to capitalize on.'

'This is great timing, Jonah. We die in a few hours and now you tell me you love me. I would have liked a few more hours to enjoy this.'

'Stop it, Jacinta. There's a reason I'm saying this now. And if I were here with another woman the conversation would be nothing like this. I want to make love to you but I want it to be right. I don't want to take advantage of you or cheapen something so beautiful. I want you to marry me. Here, in the dark of this hut, just the two of us before God, because I have finally found you.'

His voice trailed away and she realized he was serious... and how hard it must have been for him to even consider they wouldn't make it. She didn't think she had the strength to think past rise of the sun tomorrow. Now she had to.

He found her hand in the dark and stroked the inside of her palm. 'You know I love you, that I speak the truth. I never thought I would love anyone as I love you. I suddenly realized, that despite the irony and circumstances of our time together, the finding of such a love should be celebrated. I owe it to you and to myself because we should honor something so strong. For however long we live. Will you become my wife tonight?'

Would she? Could she?

Imprisoned together, and sure of death, Jonah's proposal blurred her eyes with tears. Just the two of them, in a marriage she'd never dreamt of, unpretentious yet full of symbolism for only them.

She loved Jonah, had realized that earlier and despaired of how that love would cope in their everyday lives.

But this wasn't every day. This was a filthy tent in an enemy camp and they would probably die in a few hours. She could die Jacinta McCloud or Jacinta Armstrong — avowed wife of the one man she'd ever loved and who loved her.

At least they would die together. She looked up at him and there was no denying they had found the unexpected miracle of love.

'I don't know if our marriage would work in the real world, but I do know I've fallen in love with you, Jonah.' She leaned up and kissed him. Said solemnly, 'I do love you with all my heart and I would be honored to marry you.'

He took both her hands in his and they knelt down facing each other beside the center pole. A few stars could be seen if they looked through the gap in the roof.

The first bird of the early morning woke and began calling to its mate, and although dawn hadn't broken there was less darkness in the night.

Jonah's voice came out of the dimness quietly, but a well of strength and sureness, and the shiver of goose-flesh ran down her arms at the poignancy. 'I, Jonah Gage Armstrong, here in this tent in the wilds of the New Guinea mountains, take you, Jacinta McCloud, to be my wife. To have and to hold, through richer and poorer, through sickness and in health, from this day forward, till death us do part.'

When she followed his lead and repeated the words without stumbling, he watched her steadily and his hands tightened over hers as she completed the vow.

He tugged off his sister's signet ring from his little finger and took her hand. He held her ring finger in thumb and forefinger.

'Will you wear my ring until I can buy you a proper one?' They both knew there was little chance of that happening, but it made the moment even more poignant. He slid the finely wrought ring onto her finger over her knuckle, and it rested as if sized exactly for that place on her hand.

They both stared at the symbol between them. 'I would be honored,' she whispered.

'May I kiss the bride?' he asked teasingly.

'She'd be very disappointed if you didn't.'

'Welcome, Mrs. Armstrong,' he whispered as his lips lowered to hers.

She breathed the word "husband" as she met him, determined not to shy from the hugeness of the moment.

She'd never dreamt this moment would come. She wanted it. She just hoped he didn't mind her inexperience.

He must have seen her determination because he shook his head in admiration. 'Are you afraid of anything?'

'Only of not satisfying you.' Then she tilted her chin to be honest. 'I'm no hero. I'm terrified of dying, of the morning, but we have this moment.' She lifted her hands up to circle his neck and his face came closer. 'I think you've suggested a way to keep the fear away.'

They kissed and then naturally, slowly, he unbuttoned her blouse, and the cool night air brushed her skin. Her arms goose-fleshed again, though whether from the coolness or the heat of his look she wasn't sure, but the feeling was one she savored.

He continued and slid her free of all restraints and then his own before he lay beside her on their clothes.

He rose on one elbow and with the other hand he traced the out-lines of her body. Then his mouth followed where his fingers had led until she was trembling with need. Every time she lifted her hand to touch him he settled it back by her side again and urged her to leave him to his work.

She tossed her head with the multitude of sensations and bit her lip to keep silent.

Finally he slowed and his lips returned to her face. With one searing kiss his face lifted away from her as he rose above her, and when he slowly entered her they stared into each other's eyes in the gloom until their lips met again.

Slowly he rocked and she held her breath in tiny gasps until he drove deeper and she rose to meet him. His chest rock solid against hers and the taste of his skin on her tongue – salt and something she would never forget.

That, and belonging, even briefly, to Jonah.

This moment was divinely right and she gloried in the force be-tween them and in the surging joy that rose inside her. Her body thrummed and he moaned her name in a deep whisper that teetered her on the edge until together they seemed to rise into the sky in a myriad of lights that left her shaking.

Finally her breathing slowed and she lay against him, exhausted yet more alive than she had ever been. He hugged her to him and she dozed with his strong arms around her – the constant murmurs of their guards outside ensuring there was no chance for escape.

Later, they joined once more and he stilled her cries of joy with his mouth. Softly murmuring their dreams and their secrets, they came to know each other intimately and made poignant love until the dawn began to break properly.

They even whispered of the chance that for one night they could have created life between them before they died. They dressed and all that was left was to wait for the tribesmen to come for them.

The flap pulled back and, instead of the fierce guards, Mimi burst in and gestured for Jacinta to follow her.

Jacinta heard Jonah ask questions and the old woman threw her answers over her shoulder as she hurried out, dragging Jacinta by the arm behind her. Jacinta looked back once and saw the guard pushing Jonah back inside the tent with his spear. Her heart raced with the suddenness of her summons as she hurried after the old woman.

They returned to the tent she'd been in the previous morning. Her fears for the health of the baby seemed unfounded. The tiny mite was bundled against another woman and was sucking vigorously at his foster mother's breast.

It was the newly widowed mother who needed her assistance.

Neena jerked uncontrollably on the earth floor and her eyes rolled in her head as she was thrown about with the force of the convulsions. The mound of covers shook as she jerked with the fit, and her pink lips had turned blue with the lack of respiratory effort. She needed drugs and they were back in the tent Jacinta turned to Mimi and sketched her rucksack with her hands.

'Dokkta bag. Hurry,' she said, and the meaning of her command was clear even though their languages weren't compatible. Mimi rushed off and Jacinta called after her for Jonah's help but held little hope that the she would bring him, too.

Jacinta knelt beside the young woman and tipped her firmly on her side into the recovery position because she was unable to stop the prolonged fit without medication.

It now seemed likely the reason Neena had gone into labor early had been pre-eclampsia. In the last few hours the woman's thin face had become round with fluid and Jacinta would bet her blood pressure was sky high. The damage to Neena's kidneys she didn't want to think about.

Mimi returned and thrust the rucksack at Jacinta, who took it, unsurprised that Jonah hadn't been allowed to come.

Neena's convulsions slowly stilled and her gasping breath signaled the end of one fit and a respite for everyone watching.

Eager to cannulate her before the next fit, Jacinta asked Mimi to hold Neena's hand while she inserted the intravenous line before the next convulsions made the procedure more difficult. She injected the antihypertensive and anticonvulsant and over the next half-hour they watched anxiously as the young woman's cerebral irritation decreased.

An hour later the young woman seemed to be sleeping peacefully and Jacinta left two strips of blood pressure tablets with Mimi to be issued three times a day until they ran out. It was all she could do.

Mimi tapped Jacinta on the arm and thanked her as she drew her away from the resting woman.

When they left the tent, they didn't head back across the camp but away towards the creek, and Jacinta assumed she was being allowed to wash again. She put down the bag and sluiced her arms.

The old woman seemed furtive in her movements and glanced repeatedly over her shoulder to ensure no one was watching them.

'We go now, follow creek, cross bridge, head to road, then I come back.'

Jacinta stared, open-mouthed. 'My friend. The other doctor. I can't leave without him.'

'Him dead. When get bag long time ago. He fight, they kill him. Dead.'

'Not true.' Jacinta looked back up to the camp and she saw group of men around a fallen figure. Cold fear brought the nausea to her throat. 'You're tricking me.'

'No.' She shook her wizened face sadly. 'Saw him go down with bad head. You bin good, you not die. Already took his clothes and boots. We go now, I come back quick-quick.'

Jacinta felt as though the woman was talking through a long tunnel and she could barely hear her. All she could hear were the words, 'Him dead.'

She tried to search in her mind for that sureness she'd had earlier that Jonah was alive, but now, when she needed it most, that reassurance eluded her.

Mimi darted off into the jungle alongside the creek and Jacinta stared after her in a grieving daze as she picked up the doctor's bag.

'Quick-quick,' the old woman whispered.

Time blurred for Jacinta as Mimi hurried her along barely discernible tracks at breakneck speed. She should be grateful but all she could think of was Jonah and the chance that Mimi was mistaken.

Branches slapped her cheek viciously, roots tangled around her feet as the tears rolled down her face, and time seemed to run into itself so that she didn't know if minutes or hours had passed. All through the mad rush of the day she hung onto the bag as though she wasn't letting Jonah down by carrying it.

Finally, Mimi stopped and pointed ahead. 'Road there. Walk for moon.' Then she was gone.

Jacinta stood on the edge of the jungle and the only sounds were the harsh stridor of her own breath and the crack of the undergrowth from scurrying animals and birds.

She stumbled out onto the beaten earth of the road, and all she wanted to do was lie down on the dirt and curl herself into a ball where she could go to sleep and wake up with all of this a bad dream.

Her shadow stretched behind her when she turned back towards the spot where she'd burst from the jungle. She'd never find the way back. She tried to tell herself that Jonah had ordered if she had the chance to run then he would have more chance without her.

But what if he wasn't dead?

What if he was hurt and unable to escape because of his injuries?

What if she'd gone back and been able to do something to help him escape?

She faced the sinking crescent moon above her and began to plod woodenly onward. She had little choice but she would never forgive herself for leaving.

Jonah

When Jonah woke up, he was naked and against a tree. An old woman studied him from where she crouched and he wondered if she was responsible for him still breathing. Or responsible for his lack of clothes. The pain in his head rose and fell in waves with his breathing like a swaying branding-iron behind his eyes.

He had no idea how long he'd been unconscious, or why he wasn't at Pudjip, and it hurt too much to try and remember. She gestured him to follow her.

The trek to Pudjip was long and arduous and he fell many times. Without the old woman he would have faltered long ago. When they finally came to the compound, the cries of the gatekeeper were a welcome sound but Jonah didn't stay conscious long enough to enjoy it.

A day later he woke. He opened his eyes and recognized the young American doctor's worried face.

'It's good to see you alive, Jonah. We thought you'd never come out of the jungle.'

'Why was I out in the jungle?'

'You were kidnapped by tribesmen four days ago on your way to the Sepik. The chief's son was sick and he later died.' Chuck's explanation was careful and Jonah had the impression he was trying not to upset him. 'You have a nasty head injury. What can you remember?'

Jonah closed his eyes and tried to remember the events of the last few days. But remember what? 'Not much.' Nothing, really.

Jonah forced down the panic that he should remember something incredibly important, and his voice was uneven. 'How long did you say I was missing?'

'Four days.'

Who else was with him? His team. 'Is Samuel all right? And Carla?'

'They were released.'

Thank God. He sagged. 'So it was just me?' Jonah's knuckles loosened on the bed. He needed to remember. 'Was anyone else taken when I was kidnapped?'

'There was a volunteer doctor, Jacinta McCloud, from Sydney, but she escaped and has returned to Australia. Jacinta was told you'd been killed. The poor girl was distraught.' Chuck's voice cracked at the memory.

Like Melinda. My God. Had they harmed her? 'Was she injured? How'd she get away?'

'She's fine. Some old woman she'd helped took her to the road and thankfully she was picked up by a plantation owner.'

Jonah sat up straighter. 'There was an old woman with me. She said she found me in the jungle but didn't know why I was there. Where's she?'

'We saw no one else. The gatekeeper said you stumbled out of the jungle on your own.'

Jonah sank his head in his hands. The name Jacinta McCloud struck no chord of recognition and the old woman would be long gone. He couldn't remember any of it but at least he remembered who and where he was. He'd just have to wait for his memory of those missing days to come back.

The next week saw Jonah quickly regain his strength, although he had to relearn the details of the patients that were missing from his memory.

They thought it a great joke that the doctor couldn't remember them. To make matters worse, Chuck was soon due to complete his term at Pudjip and they would be short-handed for medicos again before the next volunteers arrived.

Pressed for time and manpower, Jonah worried less about his lost memories, and when the panic came in the form of dreams and fractured scenes in the middle of the night, he fought to shake off the memories and concentrate on the day ahead. But the feeling of emotional bleakness stayed with him.

Jacinta

From the time the Jeep from a coffee plantation picked Jacinta up, all through the inquisition by the Papuan police, and even the overwhelming grief at the Pudjip hospital, reality passed in a blur.

She remembered little of the flight back to Sydney, arranged by her father's consulate friend, or being bundled into a car by her father and taken home to Burra. Her first clear memory was being held by Noni and reassured she was safe as she was tucked into bed.

Her heart wept for Jonah and half the time she wished she'd never followed Mimi from the camp, but a tiny part of her couldn't help but savor the crackle of fresh sheets against her skin, the taste of fresh coffee against her tongue, the sounds of birds outside her window. Everything that said that, against all odds, she had survived.

She couldn't help be glad to be alive, glad to be home, yet guilt weighed her down like a yoke around her shoulders that she hadn't gone back to die with Jonah. She told no one of their secret marriage because she didn't want to desecrate the memory with other people's curiosity.

She tried to imagine Jonah here in Burra or even her own home – or his – if he'd lived, working with her at Pickford's day in and day out, eating at smart restaurants, knowing they needed him at Pudjip and trapped in a life he didn't want.

The picture didn't fit but neither did it heal the grief and guilt.

Gradually, over the next few weeks, after she returned to her own home in Sydney, Jacinta came to the realization that Jonah had died doing what he wanted – risking all and accepting the dangers in that harsh land – because of his ideals.

A few weeks more and she was even able to feel privileged that she had been able to share such precious times with him, but the space in her heart where he lived still bled with the pain of her loss and she couldn't see the agony ever receding.

Seven weeks after her return to Australia, she woke to swirling nausea and a clarity of mind that left her stunned.

She hugged her stomach.

Jonah's child.

If anyone had told her that she would risk having a baby again, she would have called them a fool. But she was glad. Fiercely so. This was one thing she could do for Jonah. This way he would never leave her.

She could raise their child with the knowledge of his or her father, and in a safe and loving home. Goodness knew what her own father would say, but they would be a family.

She hugged her stomach again and her throat ached for what might have been. She refused to contemplate that her growing baby would suffer the same congenital heart problems as Olivia. She was sure her baby would be fine. Jonah's baby had to be fine.

Time dragged and she decided to return to work at Pickford's until she started maternity leave. Her time at Pudjip had certainly round-ed out her experience as an emergency doctor. She should put that knowledge to use.

Three months after her return and four weeks of Emergency Department later, Jacinta had stitched, resuscitated, set bones, and revived her life back to some semblance of order.

It was coming up to the end of her fourth work Friday and she stripped off her gloves and sluiced her hands. As she dried her fingers her gaze was caught by Jonah's ring. She'd never taken it off.

Three months she'd been back in Australia now, and he was on her mind constantly. It was almost as if she could feel his presence at her shoulder. Her eyes stung. Today was another day of grief and she glanced across to the ambulance bay as another stretcher was wheeled in.

One of the nurses signaled to Jacinta and hurriedly tossed the toweling into the bin and crossed the hallway. Her footsteps slowed until she came to a complete stop and stared down at the achingly familiar face of the man she loved.

Sweat trickled in tiny rivulets down his forehead past the rock-solid angles of his cheekbones and pooled in the crevices of his muscular neck.

Titanic rigors shook the white sheet sideways off his body and Jacinta noted the rapid rise and fall of his solid chest which seemed to stretch across the bed when she replaced the covering. She raised her finger and touched his face. Then his hard chest.

He felt real.

'You okay, Doctor?' The ambulance officer's concern was clear in his voice and Jacinta turned blindly.

'Jonah is here?'

Her words seemed to come from a long way off. The room darkened all of a sudden and Jacinta had huge trouble focusing her eyes on the man in front of her. Her breath caught in her throat.

The ambulance officer checked his chart. 'His wallet says his name is Jonah Armstrong.'

She staggered and reached out for the trolley. The ambulance officer leant out and steadied her. Her next words were a whisper. 'I'm sorry. I don't understand. I was told Jonah died in Papua New Guinea in March at the hands of rebels.'

The ambulance officer shrugged. 'Don't know anything about that. This guy was picked up from a house in Bondi.'

The words echoed eerily around in Jacinta's mind and the last thing she saw was the concerned face of the medic as she slid down the wall.

When she woke, she was on a stretcher and one of the nurses sat beside her. The administrator hovered anxiously above her. She felt sick and the room spun. She moistened dry lips. 'What happened?'

'You fainted. The nurses say you've been doing too much. Go home and rest.'

Then she remembered Jonah. 'Is it true that Dr Armstrong is here? Alive?'

The administrator nodded. 'I've checked and confirmed it's him, Jacinta. But not now. You've had a shock and are in no state to see him. Neither is he well enough for visitors.'

The administrator helped her sit up and her head swam as the blood drained from her face. 'Go home, Jacinta. One of the nurses will drive your car. She can get a taxi back. I'll phone you when your Dr Armstrong is well enough to see you.'

Jacinta had thought he was "her" Dr Armstrong. Though not legally.

But he'd been picked up from a house in Bondi. His house, no doubt. Just how long had he been there without contacting his supposed wife?

She chewed her lip to stop it trembling and swung her legs carefully over the side of the bed, then had to wait for her head to stop spinning.

Maybe he wasn't her Dr Armstrong after all.

Why hadn't Jonah contacted her? What possible reason could there be for him to not even let her know he was alive? After what they had been through together! Her thoughts circled and dipped while her head ached.

But in the scheme of things that didn't matter.

That Jonah was alive was unbelievable, wonderful. But she didn't understand.

She gingerly walked with the nurse who would take her home. Did Jonah assume she knew he was safe now? Did he think she'd left him there to die? It was all too much to comprehend.

Tucked up in bed at home after her colleague had fussed around her and finally left her in peace, Jacinta tried to make sense of why Jonah hadn't contacted her. How could he possibly have decided she wouldn't be worried?

All she could come up with was that he regretted the exact thing that Jacinta could never regret – their solemn marriage vows.

That and the fact that they'd made love – and that he'd said he loved her and would spend the rest of his life with her – had that weighed too heavily on him once they were both safe?

Which presented the problem of her pregnancy.

Her hand crept protectively over her stomach and to her disgust weak tears spilled down her cheeks. Her boss was right. She must have gone back too early because she'd never been this indecisive in her life.

A heavy inertia settled over her and a wave of dark weariness forced her to slide down into the bed. She'd sleep for an hour and her head would be clearer.

If Jonah was as sick as he was in January it would be useless to see him until tomorrow anyway.

The shining light in this mess remained. Jonah was alive!

Jacinta

When Jacinta saw Jonah the next morning, he still shuddered with the fever though he was awake. She walked across the room and lay her hand on his darkly tanned wrist. His skin burned as if someone roasted him slowly over a fire and his pulse pounded. She'd bet every muscle felt pummeled by a hammer.

His head shifted. 'Melinda?' His raspy voice tore at her heart.

She took his hand and squeezed it between both of her own. 'It's Jacinta, Jonah. Can you hear me?'

His body shuddered with rigor on the bed, but it was as if he couldn't grasp the gossamer identity of the person he'd lost.

Then he looked down at her hand resting on his wrist and miraculously he seemed to settle though his eyes fluttered shut. His respiration rate slowed and he sighed back against the headboard. His eyes still closed but his face seemed less strained. Finally, his lids fluttered and he looked at her.

Jacinta felt something break inside herself when he stared through her as if searching for someone else. He squeezed his eyes closed and then slowly opened them again. Moistened his lips. 'I'm sorry. I'm not myself at the moment.'

'That's fine.' Her voice sounded thick. She reached across and handed him the tumbler of water with the straw. Deja vu.

He pulled himself up against the back of the bed but he didn't look good. She just wanted to pull him into her chest and hug him. But it was as if he didn't know her.

How deep was his delirium?

Jacinta lifted her chin, annoyed with herself and maybe him too. 'My name is Jacinta McCloud and we spent two days kidnapped together in Papua New Guinea in March.'

She saw his confusion lift. 'Ah, March. My apologies, Dr McCloud.'

He frowned when she flinched at her name, and looked confused by the mixed signals she couldn't help sending.

He said, 'I did plan to visit you while I was in Sydney. Hoped you might be able to fill in some gaps.' He gestured wryly to the bed. 'Unfortunately, malaria waits for no man.'

She narrowed her eyes and focused on his words. 'What did you mean, "Ah, March"?'

'March, along with January and February, appears to be missing from my memory. Amnesia. I'm told I sustained a blow to the head during my...' he looked up at her and smiled '...our kidnapping, and I remember nothing much since Christmas.'

Christmas meant he didn't even remember the last time he was here. She wondered half-hysterically if he'd found his house or was staying in a hotel in Bondi.

He sat forward again, held out his hand and she could see he was trying really hard not to let his weak arm fall.

Amnesia. He didn't know who she was.

She took his hand though her own shook with shock, but the feel of his fingers around hers warmed her in a place that had been cold for too long. He looked so unwell. But he was alive. And not in any state to talk to her. If she was his doctor she wouldn't encourage visitors to stay.

'I'll come back, Jonah. I'm so happy to see you.' She bit her lip and swallowed, 'But I can see this isn't the time,' she said. 'I'll come back tomorrow, and if you're feeling better we can talk.'

The next morning when she entered his hospital room, he was standing by the window swaying with weakness.

Of course he was. Idiot. Big glorious idiot.

'Do you think you should be out of bed?'

'I was hoping you'd come,' he said, ignoring her question, and if she wasn't paying minute attention she would have missed how white his fingers were from hanging onto the window frame to stop from falling.

'How about you sit back on the bed and we can talk.'

He gave her a lopsided smile and inclined his head. With just a small misstep that had her heartrate go through the roof, he reached the bed safely and sank back into it. But his face was as white as the pillow he'd flopped back on.

'Seriously,' she said, exasperation filling the word, 'you push your body to the limit. You have to stop that.'

His brows rose at her tone though he didn't try to sit up. 'Apparently.'

She held up her hand. 'Sorry. None of my business,' but her voice cracked on the last word. She didn't even know if it would ever be her business no matter how much she wanted it to be.

Jacinta covered her mouth while she struggled for control. Stop it. He doesn't need this. She could fall apart later. 'You'll have to excuse my emotion. I thought you were dead and I'm very pleased to see you're not.'

'I'm pleased I'm not dead either,' he said quietly. 'And I'm pleased you're safe too.'

'When does your doctor say you can leave?'

'Probably tomorrow. I'm still pretty fuzzy in the head.'

She doubted it was sensible to explain anything now, then. She took a card from her purse. 'How about we leave the discussions until tomorrow? If you do get discharged, would you mind very much getting a taxi to this address. It's my house and I'll make sure you get home safely afterwards. That way we can be uninterrupted. I can even give you lunch.'

He smiled but she could see it was an effort. 'I've lived this episode of malaria before. By tomorrow I'll be better. Clearer. And no doubt I'll need lunch. I'll take you up on that offer.'

Jacinta

Jacinta paced. Chewed her nails. Re-checked the clock. She re-lived that first feel of her hand in Jonah's three days ago, the touch that had proved he wasn't a dream.

Then the solid feel of his chest under her fingers that had allowed the joy to burst through her and believe the reality of his survival.

She hadn't slept last night, but it was as if a huge stone cemented with guilt and grief had been lifted from her shoulders and scattered into a thousand pieces. She felt weightless and giddily excited when, in fact, the hardest part was still to come.

But how would she tell Jonah she was pregnant with their baby when he didn't even remember meeting her?

What of their secret marriage? The details of making love in some makeshift tent when they'd both thought they were going to die – did she describe that? She hated this indecision the pregnancy had brought her to.

She hated this whole insecure part of her life and the feeling that she wasn't in control but at the mercy of some fickle god who hadn't decided what he was going to do with them. It was like when her mother died all over again. She who prided herself on controlling her life.

Meeting Jonah had certainly taken that away.

She couldn't blame Jonah and it certainly wasn't her fault, but she did need to decide on her course of action in telling Jonah about their baby. And her father and Noni, but that was for later.

She sighed. What if Jonah thought she was tricking or trapping him into something he didn't want? The negatives began to cram her mind and she shook her head and picked up the pace of her footsteps again that she had unconsciously slowed with her fears.

Jacinta heard the doorbell and her heart skipped at what felt like twice her usual rate. When she opened the door, his finger reached to press the buzzer again. 'Hello, Jonah,' she said, and his hand froze in the act.

He looked up and she smiled because it was so wonderful to see him alive.

'I'm glad to see you because I thought you were dead.' She gestured him in. 'Sorry. I've already said that before. Stating the obvious. Make yourself at home. I'll explain it all in a minute.'

She watched him pass into the house and she could see he didn't remember that he'd been here before. He looked so tall and dear and she just wanted to feel him wrap her in his arms and tell her it had all been a bad dream – but she was beginning to see that the bad dream hadn't finished yet.

He didn't feel anything towards her. That thought poked like a sharpened stick.

When he stopped in the middle of the entry, she passed him and went ahead. 'This way.' She struggled to keep her voice normal. 'We'll sit in the den. Would you like something to drink?'

'Water would be good.' He sat where he'd sat once before and she poured him a glass from the tray she'd prepared while she'd been killing time, waiting for his arrival.

She began tentatively. 'How can I help you, Jonah?'

Jonah shook his head. 'We were so busy at Pudjip when I first returned that once I was physically well, I pushed my loss of memory away. There was no opportunity to worry about it. But now I have time to consider, it feels imperative I remember, as if there's something I need to do. So, thank you. Can you think of anything that happened that might be blocking me?'

Jacinta didn't know what to say. Her stomach sank and she tried to keep her voice level. 'Not that I can think of, but then, you were the one carrying the load of our escape and who knew exactly how precarious our existence was for a while there. The horror for me was when I was told you were dead by Mimi, the old woman who saved me.'

He sat forward at that. 'The old woman is a common denominator. I guess she's the one who saved me, too. But then she disappeared once she'd led me to the compound gate.' He took a deep breath. 'Lost time. How I escaped. So many loose ends.' He shook his head. 'You said you thought I'd been killed. How is it that no one told you I came out of the jungle the day after you left for Australia?'

Jacinta clasped one hand with the other to stop herself from fidgeting. 'I suppose there wasn't the opportunity. I came straight back to Australia. I couldn't get out of PNG fast enough when I thought you were dead, and my father and stepmother took me to Burra for a month.' She shuddered. 'Perhaps Missions Pacific thought I knew. It's been a terrible few months. If I had known of your escape, I would have been back on that plane so fast they would have missed me in customs.'

'Why?'

She stared at him and a tense silence stretched between them. Then she looked down into her own glass as if the future lay there. Because I love you. Because I would have wanted to be there for you. For us.

Slowly she listed the secondary reasons she would have returned. 'I felt guilty. Responsible for leaving. Mimi bundled me away and I should have made sure there was nothing I could do for you before I left. I wanted to go back but she kept saying you'd been killed and that they had already taken your clothes.'

The memory of that ghastly moment made her shudder and she hoped he'd understand. She looked up at him apologetically.

He smiled wryly. 'That part was true. I woke up in my birthday suit. And she was right.' He reached across and took her hand. It felt warm and real holding hers. 'You did the right thing. We did have more chance separately.'

He stroked her fingers and she stared down at his hand holding hers. Felt her heart crack open at the loss of all they had. She would not beg him to remember that he'd said he loved her or that he'd held her hand as they'd recited their vows. But, oh, how she wanted to.

Jacinta pulled her hand free and stood up, then she walked away to face out the window overlooking the road, surreptitiously wiping her eyes. 'So, do they say you'll get your memory back?'

He shook his head and shrugged. 'Is there anything else I should know?' He'd lowered his voice as if afraid of the answer.

'Nothing important. I'm glad you're feeling better now.' Her voice faltered and she smiled brightly and stepped back to hold out her right hand. 'I think I need to accept your memory is gone forever. It's not either of our faults and maybe there's some divine reason behind it.' Her heart was breaking but she forced a smile. 'Look after yourself, Jonah. I think you should go.

'I'm sorry I couldn't help bring back your memory.'

Jonah

Jonah's head spun. So that was it. He looked down at her small hand and then took her slim fingers in his own. It was suddenly hard to walk away from her.

There was more to this and he couldn't pinpoint it.

He stepped closer, leaned forward and gently touched her lips with his.

Her head jerked up and then she paused. Closed her eyes and sighed against him. For Jonah, the moment his lips touched hers he was transported back to another time with this mouth against his. He closed his eyes and wrapped his arms around the body he remembered on some different level, but it was as if it was another lifetime.

His gut kicked and he breathed in the scent and the taste of the woman in his arms. And she answered him with a moan that touched the core of him with a feeling of distant but definite homecoming.

What the heck? When he looked into her eyes he saw her tears, and he lifted his hand to brush them away as they ran down her pale cheek.

'Were we lovers?' A soft question, yet deep in his gut he knew they had been. How could he have no memory of that?

Jacinta raised her eyes to his. 'One night.'

His saw the pain and then his eyes drifted down, his gaze lingered on the slight roundness of her stomach and generous breasts. Before he could say anything she spun away to the window again.

'I think you'd better go.'

He froze as he realized how cruel he'd been. 'Forgive me, Jacinta. Dr McCloud.' He shook his head and stared at her rigid back. A solid wall against him.

What a disaster. She was right. He should go because there was a lot to think about. 'May I call again?'

Her hands mashed together. He saw she was overwrought and wished he could withdraw the pressure he'd just put on her. But he couldn't.

'I don't know. Yes. No. Just... go.'

This whole mess was nowhere near finished and he had to return. 'I'll phone you tomorrow morning.'

She didn't answer and he left her standing there with her spine straight. Yet, that very sign of outward strength signaled how difficult she found it not to bow under the pressure. It hurt to see the distress he caused but he needed to understand why she was so distraught.

For Jonah there was little sleep that night and he tossed in his bed and remembered the confusion and pain in Jacinta's eyes. He hated to think that he'd caused her misery. Maybe it would be better if he just left her in peace and returned to Pudjip.

But something was holding him back from doing that. In the brief snatches of rest Jonah's dreams were the worst they'd been. As he ran through the jungle, the branches slapped him and snakes darted away from his feet as twisted tree roots tried to catch his ankles.

He saw hands pulling a woman through the trees ahead, but he couldn't reach her. He had to find her before something terrible happened, but then it was too late. She disappeared from view after one bloodcurdling scream and he gasped upright in bed and realized it had been a nightmare.

His heart pounded.

Now that he knew they'd been lovers, there were more questions. Had they had a relationship in Sydney, in Pudjip, or when they were kidnapped?

How could he not remember? How had he come to allow her to follow him to PNG where the dangers were too great for a woman like her? It sounded more than improbable; it sounded impossible.

He wandered up to the turret room of a house he didn't remember buying and stared out at the moonlight shining on the ocean. He spun the telescope and stared out to sea. Damn this memory loss. He hated not having control over a situation, and this was so far out of his grasp he just had to go along for the ride.

Or should he run?

Jacinta

Jacinta woke late because it had taken her so long to get to sleep. The impact of being in Jonah's arms again had swept her feet out from under her and she wasn't sure how she was going to manage if he decided he didn't want to have anything to do with her or their child – but manage she would.

She would not give up on what they had.

She would make sure he knew she loved him and that he'd said he loved her. She would describe their time in the camp and, depending on his response to that, she would decide whether to tell him about their child.

But when he was facing her outside her door later that morning, the precariousness of their future frightened the life out of her. What if he'd been trying to comfort her before their impending death and had never truly loved her?

Standing on her doorstep, so tall and dear, but this morning there were differences. Today he looked determined and the purpose in his face made her wonder what decision he'd come to.

'I've thought about what happened yesterday,' Jonah said without preamble, 'and I have a few questions.'

He took a step forward and now that the moment had come, Jacinta wasn't sure she was ready for questions that required answers that meant decisions. As she debated whether to let him in, he capitalized on her indecision and stepped past her.

She followed him warily as he led the way to her den and he stood beside his chair, waiting for her to sit down first.

Heart in mouth Jacinta sank into the chair opposite. 'We'll see.'

He was frowning, as if in a struggle to pin down the elusive background to their relationship, and she felt sorry for him again.

'So I guess what I'm trying to find out is, were we in a relationship in Sydney?'

This she could answer. 'No. We barely knew each other. I looked after you in January when you had the first attack of malaria and you rang me a week later to look at a house with you.'

'Ah. The missing house. I only found the house because my solicitor had left a message at Pudjip about that. What intrigues me is why I would ask someone I barely knew to look at real estate with me.'

Jacinta raised her eyebrows. 'And your point is?'

'Why did I ask you?'

She couldn't see how this would help but she humored him. 'You said it was because when you looked at houses on your own, you felt that the owners would be more comfortable if you had a woman with you.'

He shook his head, as if he didn't believe her.

Jacinta raised her eyebrows again, skeptically this time. 'I think it was a line, Dr Armstrong. A little like, "come and see my etchings". We looked at the house, came back here for coffee, and that was the last I saw you before you met me in Hagen a month or so later.'

'So there was no relationship in Sydney.'

'As I've said.'

His eyes narrowed. 'What about in Pudjip?'

'Pudjip was work.' She remembered some of the special moments they'd shared and the gradual build-up of rapport between them. Did a kiss constitute a relationship? 'There was no physical relationship in Pudjip, but we worked well together. We developed a... friendship, of sorts.'

Still looking far from convinced, he sat back in his chair. 'Which leaves the time we were kidnapped.'

Jacinta avoided his eyes. 'As for the circumstances of our abduction, the danger in our situation certainly precipitated things before we really knew each other.'

He nodded impatiently. 'I can understand that, but we must have been drawn to each other before that. Tell me about your life, your childhood. Something might trigger a memory of what we had.'

Jacinta tilted her head and looked at him thoughtfully. 'That's fairly in-depth stuff. What are you going to tell me in exchange?'

He shrugged. 'What do you want to know?'

'About your sister and how she died. About your life growing up as a missionary child.' Jacinta ticked the points off on her fingers. 'About what you've been doing the last three months.'

'The last three months I spent in Pudjip. Working, since I was well enough to go back to work.' He leaned forward. 'Did believing we were going to die make us think we were in love?'

That was what she was worried about. That this might be true, on his side anyway. Her smile died from her face and she drew a deep breath. How to answer?

She remembered the bravery of Jonah's declaration in the tent the night before she escaped and his fearless admission about loving her.

How could those memories not give her strength? Her resolve firmed and she looked up. Met his gaze head on.

'I didn't "think" I loved you – I did grow to love the man I was abducted with. If that man's feelings have changed, then despite what we found together in those last few hours, I expect nothing from you.'

He looked at her – really he was looking into her – bringing that awful tension back into her shoulders. Because he knew she was holding something back. The Big Something.

'Thank you for your honesty.'

Jacinta could feel the tension in her burning and she knew she'd avoided the main reason.

He tilted his head. 'So why do I think there is something you're not telling me?' The bloke was like a terrier.

'I don't know.' She glanced down at the table. 'What makes you think there is?'

'You've been incredibly open about your feelings, but I know there's something else.'

She couldn't meet his eyes.

'See,' he said. 'That's just what I mean. You're an open and honest person – that's what I see when I look at you. But when you avoid a subject you look away.'

'Maybe I'm bored?'

'Or lying?'

Jacinta really didn't think she could stand any more dissection of her shredded feelings. 'I think you'd better leave. I've tried to be honest and you've given me nothing but a dodgy character assessment based on what? Half an hour, at most, of time you remember spending in my company. How can you know if I'm honest and open or avoiding a subject if you don't remember me? I've laid myself open for what I thought to be a good reason. I haven't lied to you.'

She may not have told him the whole truth, yet, but she hadn't told any untruths. And to back that up, she looked right at him. Into those distressingly beautiful deep blue eyes.

'I'm sorry, Jacinta. I'm thirty-seven years old and I've always—' he stopped, ran his hand through his hair '—always planned to remain single, and I can't believe I intended to hurt you. I don't understand. I'm too old to change my ways. I love my job and it's too dangerous to have a family. I'm used to travelling light.

'I promised, when my sister died...' His voice had dropped, but what he said was very clear. 'I promised that I would never risk another woman's life because she loved me and wanted to be with me. I don't know what I was thinking during our capture, but at this moment I must stand by beliefs I've held for ten years. I have nothing to offer you. Unless I remember why I must change, there's no future in a relationship between us.'

Jacinta closed her eyes for an agonized few seconds as she tried to gather her thoughts. So that's it, then. Couldn't get any clearer. It was no more or less than she'd told herself in the tent all those weeks ago.

She reminded herself that she loved this man, but he didn't want to love any woman enough to risk his own pain if anything happened to her.

Her stomach reacted in protest. She needed some food for her churning stomach and her head had begun to ache. Either way, she couldn't face Jonah Armstrong any more at this moment.

Bracing herself against the pain, Jacinta opened her eyes for one last look at him. Then tugged at the signet ring he'd given her. 'This is yours.'

His eyes widened. 'How did you get that? I thought the men had stolen it when they took my clothes.'

'You gave it to me for safekeeping.' She looked away. 'Perhaps you could show yourself out.'

Jacinta left him standing there and ran up the stairs to the safety of her room, where she shut the door and leaned against it. She was a mess, mentally and physically, and Jonah's presence only made it worse. Knowing he lived just a short drive away made it worse.

She wanted Noni and her father. She wanted distance between her and Jonah and freedom from decisions made in the heat of the moment. She didn't know if withholding the truth was the right thing but she couldn't take much more.

Jonah

Jonah walked down Jacinta's front steps and stared at the ring. It was still warm from her finger. He was glad to be outside because suddenly his head thumped with a sharp pain and his vision blurred. His sister's ring cut into his palm as he clenched his fist and tried to contain the explosion happening in his head.

He drove home carefully, crawled into bed and pulled the covers over his head to block out the light. He hoped like hell he wasn't coming down with malaria again, though it didn't feel like that.

These symptoms were different, and the pain increased until he screwed up his face and moaned. Then everything went black.

When he surfaced hours later, Jonah was so close to remembering that he didn't want to return to reality. He fought against waking up.

Slowly, in the mists, it was as if Jacinta was there and she slid her hands down his chest and he just wanted her skin against his. 'You are so beautiful,' he murmured as his lips brushed one creamy shoulder.

'Make love to me, Jonah. So I can know you are real and we are both really here.'

She reached for him and then they were both naked and together on the thick carpet, Jacinta in his arms, her skin like silk, soft strands of hair against his chest.

He rolled over onto his back, bringing her with him, until she stared down at him and he could drink in the sight of her, with her black hair hanging each side of her face and her dark eyes burning into his.

He reached up to cup her face but suddenly she was gone again.

There was no one above him and when he woke he realized she was the angel of his dreams.

The pain in his head had eased but the one in his heart had grown. Even though his memory had not returned, he knew Jacinta was everything he wanted in a woman and everything he refused to risk.

Many hours later, when he finally slept again, he dreamt of the horror of Melinda's death.

In the morning he knew his decision to leave Jacinta safe had been the right one.

Jonah woke with the sun. His headache a dull reminder now, he swung his feet to the floor and waited for the giddiness to pass before he turned his head to glance at the clock.

It was early yet, but she might be an early riser. He was about to find out.

He paused while pulling on his shoes. He wondered if she'd even talk to him after his last visit when he'd worn out his welcome well and truly.

He needed to tell her he would return to Pudjip.

He owed her that much.

The drive to Jacinta's house took less time than it should have, but there were no signs of life in the house.

When he rang the doorbell nobody answered.

Jonah stepped back and tried to see inside the windows, but they all seemed to be shut with blinds drawn.

Had she left already, or was she inside but pretending she wasn't home?

No. She wasn't the type to cower behind curtains and pretend absence.

Jonah shook his head, mocking himself for making – in her words – another dodgy character assessment. If she's gone away to escape seeing him again, it was for the best.

He returned to his car and drove home to pack his bags for Pudjip.

Jacinta

Jacinta climbed out of the car after the six-hour drive to Burra and her family. Iain McCloud, his wife Noni, and even Noni's Aunt Win had come over from her own house with her husband. They were all there to greet her.

'Hello, Jaz. Welcome home.' Her father dropped a kiss on the top of her head, Noni reached up to hug her, and Aunt Win folded her in her arms and spun her around. Jacinta realized she'd come to the right place.

'It's good to be here.' The mob ushered her inside and Jacinta could feel the tension easing away from her neck as unconditional love and support surrounded her.

She felt seventeen again, except now she gladly accepted that others would care for her until she recouped her stamina. Her shoulders slumped with pleasant weariness and she sank into the chair in the study. It was so good to have her family around her.

'You need rest and fattening up, young woman.' Aunt Win had taken one look at her and given her usual diagnosis.

Jacinta met Noni's eyes around the elderly lady's not inconsiderable girth and smiled. Aunt Win was known for trying to fatten people up and she bustled away, no doubt to fetch a laden tea tray even though she wasn't the housekeeper here anymore.

Iain and Noni sat together on the lounge and Iain draped his arm around his wife's shoulders and absently stroked her arm with his fingers. Since their marriage twelve years ago, Iain's adoration of his second wife had only grown.

Jacinta couldn't help a trickle of self-pity when she thought of what it would mean to have Jonah sit in such a way with her. Now or twelve years in the future. Either would do.

Noni handed her a cup. 'Now, tell us how you really are.'

Jacinta sighed back in the chair. 'I'm tired and confused and I don't know which way to go, so I thought I'd come home for a day or two to sort out my head.'

There was a small silence and Noni said quietly, 'You made the right choice to come home. It was wonderful news that Jonah escaped as well. We couldn't believe it when you rang us. You said you were going to see him. How does he look?'

'He looks well.' She looked down into her cup. 'Thin but fabulous, actually.'

Noni and Iain exchanged a look that Jacinta pretended not to see and she went on, 'He's suffered a head injury and lost the last three months of his memory before our kidnapping. He doesn't remember me or the kidnapping.'

Iain's interest sharpened. 'Focal amnesia, eh?' He chose a plump brown scone and bit into it without noticing the warning look his wife sent. 'Tricky. Never know which way that will go.'

Noni and Aunt Win both glared at him.

Iain caught the tail end of his wife's displeasure and raised his eyebrows. 'What?'

'Obviously you're interested in the technical side, darling,' Noni said before turning back to Jacinta. Her voice gentled. 'It must have been hard for you when you first saw him.'

Aunt Win leaned across and squeezed Jacinta's knee.

Noni smiled sideways at her husband. 'People do get their memory back, don't they, Iain?'

Not slow to take a hint, Iain nodded his agreement. 'Is he having flashbacks?'

Jacinta sighed. 'I don't know. If I see him again, I'll ask him.' She swallowed the lump in her throat. 'Though I might not see him again.' She opened her mouth to say something else but looked at her father and clamped her lips shut.

Noni winked at her husband and jerked her head towards the door. He raised his eyebrows as if to say, I don't understand, and Noni pretended to glare.

Slightly slow to take this hint, Iain grinned and stood up. 'Excuse me, Jaz. I've remembered I need to make a phone call. I'll be back soon.'

He squeezed his daughter's shoulder as he passed and Aunt Win stood up as well. 'Just going to pop the pie I brought over into the oven,' she said to no one in particular as she followed Iain from the room.

Jacinta looked at Noni and grimaced. 'That was subtle.'

'Your father doesn't know subtle.' Noni patted the seat beside her. 'Come and sit over here, Jaz.'

Jacinta moved across and sank onto the lounge beside Noni, who put her arm around her.

'There's more to this than what you told us last time you were here.'

Jacinta leaned into Noni's hug and rested her head as she dashed a hand across her eyes. 'That I'm a grown woman and I'm acting like a clueless teenager? I love Jonah so much it hurts.'

She looked at Noni, and her stepmother nodded. 'I remember that all too well.'

'I knew you'd understand. We fell in love while we were kidnapped. Well...' She qualified the statement. 'It grew from the first moment we saw each other. He said that, too, and now his memory of it all is gone.'

'Oh, my love. You poor thing. Does he remember anything about the two of you?'

'He remembered he'd kissed me before when he kissed me yesterday.'

Noni smiled gently. 'That sounds promising.'

Jacinta gave a bitter little laugh. 'That's what I thought. But it's not enough. He loves his work. He's an amazing man. But he lost his sister to rebels in New Guinea and says he'll never risk another woman's life. That he'll always be single and there's no future for us.'

Noni sat back. 'That's not good news if you love him.'

Jacinta turned her head and looked at Noni. 'Especially as I'm pregnant.'

Noni pursed her lips and squeezed Jacinta's hand. 'Does he know?'

Jacinta shook her head.

'Tricky.' Noni offered her husband's favorite word and they both laughed.

Jacinta sighed again but this time there was that flicker of hope. Things did work out. Maybe it was just going to take time. Just talking to Noni about it helped.

'What do you want to do, Jaz?'

'I'll stay tonight but I think I've decided to go back to Sydney to find Jonah.' She said it slowly but the plan took shape as she uttered the words. 'If he's already gone, then I'll follow him to Papua New Guinea. He'll be cross but I can deal with that. He was cross last time and he changed. Maybe me being there will help his memory return.'

'And what are you going to tell him when you find him?'

Her voice shook. 'Nothing about our baby yet because it would color his decision.' Then she strengthened. 'I'm going to do the work I went there to do for the few more weeks I have left before my pregnancy shows, prove that I can handle the life and just be thankful that Jonah isn't dead.' She looked at Noni. 'The rest is up to him.'

'So you'd go back to Papua New Guinea and work again in the hospital? Do you want to do that?' Noni looked at Jacinta searchingly, compassion and worry at war in her eyes.

'I want to. I loved the work and the people. But I will come home to Burra to have my baby. I know I have to do that.'

Noni hugged Jacinta and tears stung as they both thought of Jacinta's last tiny baby born here. 'I can understand why you want to do that.'

There was risk. 'If I get sick, will you make sure I get home?'

Noni smiled. 'I have no doubt your father and his friends will make that happen.'

Something bumped against the wall outside the door and they smiled at each other.

Noni rolled her eyes. 'You can come in, Iain.'

'Oh, Jaz, you're pregnant?' He didn't even try to pretend he hadn't been listening. He hugged her and then stepped back, spreading his hands. 'Are you feeling okay? You're well?'

Jacinta leaned up and kissed his cheek. 'Yes, Dad. I'm well.'

'So what's this fellow's name? What sort of missionary doctor is he, anyway, getting my daughter pregnant while she does volunteer work?'

Agitated again, Iain took a turn around the room and Noni and Jacinta watched him let off steam without saying a word. They'd seen it all before.

He flung out his hand and looked at his wife. 'Can't he see she's struggled so hard to get where she is today? Now she's back at the beginning again.'

Jacinta winced.

'No, she's not.' Noni judged the time was right to have her say. 'Jacinta is a capable career woman and an amazing doctor. We know she's a fabulous mother. If she and Jonah don't end up together, she will manage beautifully. The fact that she loves a man who doesn't know he loves her is the problem, not her pregnancy.'

'Jonah!' Iain scowled. 'He's Jonah'd my daughter, that's what he's done.'

Noni laughed softly and stood up and planted her feet in her husband's way so that he had to stop pacing. 'Now, remember that the path of true love is often difficult. I don't believe Jacinta would fall in love with an unworthy man.'

The older couple stopped and turned to her. Her father asked, 'Is that right, Jacinta?'

She smiled, feeling more settled in her decision with every minute that passed. 'Oh, he's worthy. Just doesn't remember that I'm the woman for him yet.'

But watching the indulgent love between Noni and her dad made her remember love was worth fighting for.

Noni leaned up and kissed Iain. 'They are probably as in love as we are even after all these years.'

Iain looked down at his diminutive wife and his face and voice softened. 'Oh, they couldn't be that much in love.' He kissed her back before returning to the topic at hand. 'All right. So, the guy didn't mean to get amnesia and maybe Jaz consented to sleep with him, but why hasn't he followed her here? Even if just to find out why he feels weird about her?'

'We tried that,' Jacinta said dryly and reached for the food. Suddenly her appetite was back.

'He's probably as confused as she is. Give him time. Give them both time. And—' Noni poked her husband gently in the chest with one finger '—if he does turn up here, I want you to be the charming man I know you can be. Not some irate father who's forgotten that his daughter is nearly thirty years old and not seventeen.'

Ian stopped and stroked his wife's cheek. 'Yes, dear.' They smiled at each other. 'What would we do without you?'

'Talk to your daughter. I'm going to find Aunt Win.' She looked back. 'I don't know what you would do, but I'd be lost.'

She blew her husband a kiss and trotted away, and Jaz shook her head at the wolf whistle that followed her.

Jonah

Jonah heard the Jeep drive in to Pudjip and his hand froze in the act of writing. Jacinta must have pulled some hefty political strings because he'd been trying his hardest to keep her in Australia.

He had no idea of the real reason behind Jacinta McCloud's arrival, only that she'd told Missions Pacific she'd be staying for a month to make up for the time she hadn't completed. He would have to count down the days until the torture was finally over.

The patient chart beneath his fingers seemed to fade as he stared through it, searching for the right path to take.

She was here – the woman he could only remember meeting twice – but whose presence still dominated his thoughts and his dreams. He had no idea how his confusion had come to this and he'd ended up in a situation he'd always sworn he would avoid.

A few minutes later her quiet footsteps entered his tiny office and he put the pen down.

'Hello, Jonah.' Jacinta's voice drifted across the room to him like a siren's call, and slowly he lifted his eyes to drink her in.

She was even more beautiful than he remembered.

Her dark eyes seemed to see right through him, and the determination in her face told him there was nothing he could say to make her leave. Which meant he had to accept she would see out her term and it was up to him to keep her safe.

'Dr McCloud.' He stood up and she crossed the room to shake his hand. He hesitated but she stood in front of him with hand outstretched and he had no choice.

Ah, Jacinta, he thought, you don't know how dangerous this is.

Her fingers were warm and wonderful beneath his.

'You look well,' he said. And she did. Her cheeks glowed pink and her black hair shone lustrously in the poor light of his office. She'd gained a little weight and even her breasts looked rounder. He dragged his eyes away from her body to the doorway behind her to ground himself.

He needed her outside this room because in this relative privacy he was tempted to recapture the elusive magic he'd felt that day in her house with his arms around her and his lips against hers.

Since returning to Pudjip it had been even harder than he'd feared to put aside the few memories he did have of Jacinta.

He straightened. The only solution was to treat her like any other volunteer. 'Right. Let's get you orientated and the safety briefings done.'

'I have been here before, Jonah,' she said quietly, and he realized that, of course, this was true.

His brain was fried and she'd only just got here. 'Then come and say hello to Carla and Samuel.'

She followed him as he left the office, and he breathed a sigh of relief until she laughed softly.

'That's funny,' she said from behind his shoulder. 'Samuel told me it was you who asked him to pick me up. So I've already spent a few hours with him.'

He'd forgotten the arrangements he'd put in place for her arrival, and he couldn't blame the amnesia. The woman made him crazy in a way he'd never been crazy before.

The best thing he could do was put her to work. There was always enough of that.

Jacinta

Jacinta followed him and for the moment she was content to just settle in.

The sight of him, so tall and vital, soothed the part of her that still woke sweating with memories of when she thought he'd died. He seemed a little distracted and she wondered if her arrival had unsettled him. She hoped so.

She hung back a little just to savour the sight of his strong shoulders and broad back, which she remembered so vividly beneath her hands. The thrill of excitement she'd been trying to keep in check grew in her stomach. He was her man and she had done the right thing to come here to fight for him.

She caught up, and as they crossed the ward, Jacinta's gaze rested on a small boy who was wriggling around on his bed like a happy fish, all eyes and wide smile as he tried to catch her attention.

'Peeta!' She left Jonah and swept the little boy into her arms and hugged him. 'You look so big.'

'Me big and muscles.' The boy flexed his skinny arms importantly and Jacinta laughed. She tousled his hair and stood up. 'I come back, quick-quick, you wait.'

She'd brought a tiny red fire engine in her luggage from Sydney in case Peeta was back again as an inpatient. It had been the memory of his smiling face that had helped her remember the reason they had been in Papua New Guinea. The reason for the life Jonah had chosen.

Over the next few hours Jacinta slipped into the routine as if she'd never left, and she marveled again at how calm and caring Jonah was with his patients. This was where he belonged. She just needed him to see that she belonged by his side.

Days and then two weeks passed, and she'd graduated into looser tops and baggier pants. She didn't think anyone would notice the tiny bulge that proclaimed her condition, although she had seen Carla nod to herself.

Suddenly she found herself alone with Jonah more often, as first Carla and then Samuel seemed to find other things to do when the three or four of them ended up working together. Once she caught Carla's knowing smile and it felt good to have an ally.

Gradually Jonah softened, as she knew his fairness would make him do. They shared a few jokes and he soon began to meet her eyes at crucial moments in patient care as if to share the burden with her.

That was why she was here. Not just for herself and her baby but because Jonah needed to share the weight of his responsibilities. But he didn't say anything. It was as if the evolution of his feelings was happening without his consent and he refused to acknowledge them.

By the third week they were at stalemate. Jacinta loved him more than ever and she didn't think he was immune to her, but she began to fear he would never change his mind. His reservations for her safety would never allow her to stay, and she began to wonder if she had the right to force him. The last days passed swiftly and the distance Jonah had placed between them remained as unbreachable as it had been when Jacinta first arrived, at least on the outside.

Jacinta's quandary was her pregnancy. She hadn't wanted to influence Jonah's decision with such a weapon, but now she held little hope he would ask her to stay. It was his right to know he was to be a father before she left.

Yet the right moment to share her news never seemed to materialize. The day before she left finally dawned and she could wait no longer.

Carla and Samuel stood up as Jonah entered the communal dining room and again they left the two of them to eat together. There was something different about Jonah today, she thought as she glanced across the table. Her skin prickled with unease.

'Last day and you'll be back in civilization.'

Jacinta thought his eyes softened when he looked at her but he was talking openly about her impending departure. She needed to break the news to him. 'I need to talk to you, Jonah. It's important. Will you listen now?'

He looked at her and something flickered in his eyes that belied his nod. 'Sure,' he said.

But then Carla rushed in and called him and Jacinta watched him hurry off. She sighed. Maybe tonight would be better.

Another busy day passed. The shadows of dusk were growing when the young woman approached the gatekeeper and asked for Missy-Dokkta.

When the message came, Jacinta looked across the ward at Jonah, his head bent over the patient he was talking to, and she wondered if she could slip away without him seeing. He would be livid if he knew she was talking to someone outside the compound.

As she approached the gate she recognized the young mother from the kidnappers' rebel camp.

'Is your baby sick, Neena?'

Neena shook her dark hair. 'Mimi sick. Mimi die if Missy-Dokkta not come.'

Jacinta frowned. 'Bring Mimi to hospital. Much better.'

'Mimi not come till Missy-Dokkta say okay. Not get in trouble.'

'Mimi's not in trouble. Mimi is my friend.'

'You come tell her that.'

Jacinta shook her head. She wasn't that stupid. 'I'm not going back to Mimi's camp.'

'Meet just little way away. Then Mimi come.'

'I'm not allowed to leave the compound.'

'We be quick-quick.'

'Not that quick, Neena. I ask Dokkta to come and talk to you.'

'No. Dokkta not come. Missy-Dokkta safe.'

The impasse was real and Jacinta chewed her finger. She could not forget that Mimi had not only saved her life but the life of Jonah as well. Jacinta didn't believe that Neena would cause her harm either. She wanted to help her if she could. If they were quick she could be back before Jonah knew she was gone.

If he discovered she'd left there would be hell to pay. But then a little hell might be worth it because she was sick of this wall of politeness he'd erected.

She held up a finger to Neena. 'One minute.'

She hurried to pack an emergency medical bag and slipped out the gate.

Jonah

For Jonah, it was the day before the one he dreaded and a day he longed for. She seemed everywhere. Even without the earlier memories, she infiltrated his thoughts as he sutured torn skin, welcomed new babies, and set bones that had broken. He knew he had to make her leave before he weakened and took her in his arms again.

There seemed so much magic associated with Jacinta as he watched her work. He had to keep reminding himself that his way had always been alone, that the events of March only highlighted the danger to her and strengthened his resolve.

All he could do was try not to be alone with her. Thank goodness for work.

'Where's Dr McCloud?'

Jonah entered the dining room a little after six and was surprised to see Jacinta's place at the table still vacant. Carla looked up from the bowl of vegetables she was dishing out and glanced around.

She met her husband's eyes and Samuel shrugged denial of any knowledge of Jacinta's whereabouts. 'We thought she was with you.'

Jonah glanced at his watch and his unease deepened. 'I haven't seen her for an hour or so.'

Carla frowned at the concern in his voice. 'She's probably in her hut. I'll go and look for her.'

Jonah shook his head. 'You stay and have your meal. I'll go.'

Jonah stamped down the panic that had appeared out of nowhere. There was no reason for him to think that anything had happened to Jacinta. She was only late for a meal, which was something he was often guilty of.

He checked her room, but there was no answer when he knocked. He tried again and then went along to check the communal bathroom and the long ward of the hospital. The evening shift hadn't seen her.

Finally, he skirted the building and poked his head into the labor ward. Still no sign of Jacinta. The casualty room lay in darkness so she wasn't in there, either, and the feeling of unease that was growing inside him brought a cold sweat to his brow.

The walk to the gatehouse was the longest walk of his life. His heart thumped in his chest, and he prayed the whole way that she hadn't left the compound. When he reached the gatekeeper's hut he pounded on the door with enough force to propel the keeper out of his chair and onto the floor. The little man picked himself up and hurried to the door.

'Have you seen Dr McCloud?'

'Missy-Dokkta left Pudjip with tribal woman one hour ago.'

Jonah felt the gaping chasm of his worst fears open beneath him. 'How did she leave?'

'On foot.'

Just like Melinda.

Suddenly his head split with pain and nausea rose in his throat, the same nausea as the day Jacinta had given him back the ring.

He looked down at his hand and his sister's ring and the butterfly cut into his palm as he clenched his fist and tried to shut out the agony inside his head. But the wave of pain increased until he screwed up his face and moaned.

Everything went black.

When he woke, the kaleidoscope of the last few months streamed past in his mind with a clarity that stunned him. His trip to Sydney, the malaria and meeting Jacinta, the two of them at his house and even her first arrival in Mt Hagen – all there in technicolor detail.

He remembered the tense nights of the kidnapping and the final morning after their symbolic marriage, the glory and fear when he'd been sure they would both die that day. Then the run of images wound down and he lived the next memories second by second.

His heart rate accelerated and cold sweat broke out on his brow again as he relived his terror when Jacinta had left the tent with Mimi the second time.

He hadn't trusted them.

It had been too close to sunrise and the promise of death. He'd needed to take Jacinta from there or something bad would be unavoidable.

He'd dug the knife quickly from beneath the post and stepped to the rear of the tent where he'd slit the tough canvas to make a hole big enough to escape through as soon as Jacinta returned. Then the old woman had reappeared without her.

'Dokkta lady want medicines.' Mimi had snatched up the bag and the guard had gestured for Jonah to step back while she'd left the tent.

That was when the guard said he would be having big sport with the dokkta's woman when the sun rose.

Jonah didn't remember how his hands came to be around the throat of the guard, but a searing pain and a flash of light as another guard hit him – he remembered that. Along with the cold shock of realization that he hadn't saved Jacinta.

Then nothing, until he awoke beside the tree with the old woman.

Obviously the guards must have thought him dead. Either way, they had left him, and with Mimi's help he'd escaped.

As had Jacinta.

He twisted in the bed and forced his eyes open. Jacinta, his wife, was out there in the jungle and he needed to find her.

'Can you hear me, Jonah?'

Her voice.

He turned his head and there she was. He lifted her fingers to his lips and that pulled her towards him, staring into the eyes of the woman he loved more than life itself. He saw her concern and her love and her fear of rejection again.

Her black hair hung each side of her face like in the dream, and her chest rose and fell with her rapid breathing. She must have hurried to be here. He shook his head at the paleness of her features and sat up on the edge of the bed. 'You're back.'

She smiled. 'Yes. I'll always come back because we are a part of each other.'

'Why did you leave?'

'Some risks must be taken.' She thought of the risk of his anger and that he would still send her away tomorrow if he was unwilling to face his own fears. 'Mimi needed me and now we can look after her like she looked after us.'

'And will you look after me like you have before?'

He pulled his sister's ring from his finger and it lay in his palm for a moment as they both stared at it. Then he slipped it onto the ring finger of her left hand.

'You remember?' she said, and her eyes filled with tears of joy. 'Your memory is back?'

'My poor, darling wife.' He pulled her close against his chest and for the first time in months he felt alive. Truly and utterly alive. 'I remember everything, and I'm so sorry you had to go through that.'

He caught her other hand and her fingers looked so small in his.

'I remember I love you and want to spend the rest of my life with you.'

She stepped back out of his arms and looked up at him. He could see she wanted to believe him, but something was holding her back. 'So what dark and dreadful memory stopped you from remembering that before? Why were you so frightened of remembering me?'

He wasn't proud of his behavior but she deserved the truth. 'When I discovered you'd left the compound today, the shock and memory of what happened to Melinda shattered the memory block my fears had created.' He sighed. 'I heard them planning to ambush you on the way back with Mimi.' He shook his head and the expression on his face gave him away. 'I had to stop them going for you.' Unconsciously his hands tightened on hers. 'And the last thing I remembered was that I'd failed. I hadn't saved you.'

She'd always known he was more concerned about her fate than his own. It made sense if he believed that she had died a horrible death just like his sister.

Jacinta remembered what he'd said that day in her house. He would never risk another woman's life because she loved him.

She pulled her hands free and looked up at him, and she knew he could see the indecision in her face. 'How will you cope if we have a family? Where will we live? What about your love of Pudjip? Because if you work here, I'm staying with you.'

He pulled her slowly back against him and stared down into her courageous face. 'A family with you I would adore. You mean everything to me and I can help Pudjip in other ways as well. Missions Pacific have wanted me to lecture for them for years to raise awareness of our plight and need for funds.' He cupped her cheek in his hand. 'I want to live my life with you. For the last few years I've only existed, and I never dreamt I would find a woman like you. You have such strength and humor and you make me appreciate things I forgot to appreciate years ago.'

Jacinta kissed the hand that lay beside her mouth. 'You would have to let me share responsibility, share your burdens. I won't be left on the outside because I'm your wife.'

He nodded. 'You could give the woman's perspective on medicine in the developing world. You and I could travel the world seeking sponsors and do occasional stints here at the hospital if that's what we want, or in Sydney.'

'You have it all worked out.'

'Marry me,' he said.

Finally she softened. 'I'm already married.' She smiled as she reached up and kissed him. 'I died inside when I thought you were dead, and it was so hard not to plead with you to love me when you came back and your memory was gone.'

'Let me show you how much I love you.' He looked around at the interested ward and laughed out loud. 'But not here.'

She helped him stand and together they smiled at the caring faces around them.

'Missy-Dokkta now Mrs-Dokkta,' he said mock-seriously to his patients. Then he took her hand as if he would never let her go and they left the ward together.

In his room, he kissed her and wrapped his arms around the woman he'd never thought would hold him like this again. He savored the softness and vitality that he'd thought were gone for ever.

Later, when they parted, she smiled and looked up into his face. 'And did you suspect I have more news to tell?'

He frowned, his mind sluggish with desire, until her meaning burst into his consciousness. A feeling of awe swept over him and he ran his hand gently over the growing bulge in her stomach.

'My child?'

'Our child.' She leaned up and kissed him. 'Pudjip's child.'

His face softened as he thought of sharing a new life with his love. 'And what shall we call our baby?'

'We'll have to check with her, but I'd like to call our child Mimi.'

Jonah laughed. 'And if he's a boy?'

'His middle name can be Mimi.'

Jonah

Two months later.

The wedding was held at Burra and the father of the bride sat down after handing over his daughter.

Iain admired the towering tent his daughter and new son-in-law had hired from the circus, though why they couldn't have had an ordinary marquee he didn't understand.

He had to admit, though, that the huge central pole was impressive, with vines that travelled to the roof and luminous stars adorning the apex. But he wasn't sure about the symbolic dower chains that tied the bride and groom together.

'Didn't you see the movie Braveheart, Iain?' Noni thought it all very romantic and she squeezed her husband's hand. 'When William Wallace married his lady in the woods with only the preacher?'

Iain lifted his wife's hand to his lips and kissed her palm. 'Must have missed it. Jacinta looks gorgeous, doesn't she?' Iain whispered proudly as his daughter renewed her vows in a voice that carried clearly to the rear of the assembly. The flowing white dress fell from beneath the square lace bodice to pool at her feet and she looked like a joyful forest goddess. The looseness of the material shifting in the slight breeze briefly outlined the swell of the baby yet to be born.

In the center of the tent, Jonah heard his new father-in-law and agreed. His wife. His dearest love. He stared down into Jacinta's eyes and remembered another exchange of vows with the same tenderness shining up at him from Jacinta's face.

He could barely believe the joy in his heart and the certainty that their life ahead together would be beyond anything he had ever imagined now that he had Jacinta beside him.

With their vows renewed in front of family and friends, Jonah and Jacinta turned to face the congregation.

This time light and beauty and new adventures stretched ahead of them and they both savored their unknown future as they gently kissed.

Jonah raised Jacinta's hand bound to his and Melinda's signet ring flashed in the light, along with the diamond beside it. 'I introduce you to my wife, Jacinta Armstrong.' His voice rang deep and clear and full of pride, and the congregation rose as one and cheered.

As they descended into the throng, Jonah held firmly to his wife's hand and his heart sang as she squeezed his fingers joyfully back. He knew they held the most precious gift between them.

Neither saw the two tiny blue butterflies that hovered above them in blessing before soaring off into the sunlight, but he could feel the love inside him swell.